21/10/ 18

WAT

Please renew or return items by the date
shown on your receipt

www.hertfordshire.gov.uk/libraries

Renewals and enquiries: 0300 123 4049

Textphone for hearing or 0300 123 4041
speech impaired users:

Hertfordshire

L32 11.16

SPIRIT

www.**davidficklingbooks**.com

SPIRIT

Sally Christie

David Fickling Books

31 Beaumont Street
Oxford OX1 2NP, UK

Spirit
is a
DAVID FICKLING BOOK

First published in Great Britain in 2018 by
David Fickling Books,
31 Beaumont Street,
Oxford, OX1 2NP

978-1-910989-30-2

1 3 5 7 9 10 8 6 4 2

Papers used by David Fickling Books are from
well-managed forests and other responsible sources.

DAVID FICKLING BOOKS Reg. No. 8340307

A CIP catalogue record for this book is available from the British Library

Typeset in 11/18pt Sabon by Falcon Oast Graphic Art Ltd.
Printed and bound in Great Britain by Clays Ltd, St Ives plc

To Celia
for connectedness

Chapter 1

THE TRUTH GAME

'I saw a real live fairy,' he said, 'and I took it home in a bag.'

Well, what would *you* think if someone said that? If it was someone you knew – a friend – you might say they were joking. But nobody knew Matt Barker. No one could guess why he'd said what he'd said. Was he attention-seeking? Was he a show-off? He didn't look the type.

They wanted to laugh, but that was against the rules. You had to respect what anyone said. And yet they felt *he* was laughing at *them*. Was he trying to make them look stupid? Taking advantage?

The one thing they knew for certain was he wasn't telling the truth.

And that was the problem. In the Truth Game, you had to. If you chose to open your mouth (and you might well not, but if you did) the rule was that any words that came out of it had to be true. If people broke that, then they'd better not play. As Mr McGann was fond of saying, he could equally well have called it the Trust Game – because truth and trust are so closely connected.

When Mikey Maloney had told them last term he'd done seventy-nine keepy-uppies, round the back of his house, they'd all had to trust that he really had (he had) because no one – not even Dip Jay or Joe Black – had been there. And when Angela Poole had chosen to say that she'd watched her grandpa actually die, she was trusting them to be understanding and ask only sensitive questions. They did, but even so Ange started crying and Mr McGann stopped the game.

He had a right to do that. He could do that now. But he didn't want the new boy to think that that was all there was to it. He could feel the anger around him, and several people had put up their hands.

Joe Black, a nice enough lad, thought Mr McGann,

but sparky: what would he ask? Something challenging. Something to show he was nobody's fool. *This fairy, where did you find it, then? How did you catch it?*

Tasha, who led the girls, what would she? *This 'fairy' of yours, what's it like?*

Neither would do, thought Mr McGann. Matt Barker mustn't be confronted. Gently, within the rules of the game, he had to be given a way out. But all the hands going up now were hostile. Till Angela raised hers.

Angela Poole was known for her kindness. Mr McGann had to chance it.

'Angela,' he said, 'this is a tricky one.'

Angela Poole would do what was best.

'Go on, then, Angela. What is your question?'

Angela asked it slowly and carefully. 'So, what you're saying is, really and truly, you've got a real, live – fairy – at home? I'm just checking I've got that right.'

Matt Barker should have been grateful. Mr McGann was – but then, he'd invented the game and didn't want it wrecked. But when Matt Barker answered Angela Poole, you couldn't tell what he was feeling.

'No,' he said.

That was all. A retreat as mysterious as his opening line. But the situation was saved.

'Well done, Matt!' said Mr McGann. 'The thing in this game is to tell the truth.' Relief made him speak a little too loudly. 'You'll get used to it after a while –' hearty laugh – 'and you'll realise how interesting it can be. Now, that's it for the moment, everyone. I must go and see Spike.'

Spike was the driver of the coach they were on, and right now he was changing a wheel. In the middle of France, on Day Two of their trip, they'd managed to get a flat tyre. They were stuck in the lay-by half an hour more, but they didn't go on with the Truth Game. You had to be in the right mood for that, and Matt Barker had spoiled it. They sang songs instead: mostly 'WHY ARE WE WAITING?'

Mr McGann said, 'You *know* why we're waiting!' but they sang it anyway.

Next day, on the way to the goats' cheese farm, the road had lots of twists and bends and, one by one, people began feeling sick. Angela actually was sick, and the smell made everything worse. ('Wait till we get to the farm,' said Mr McGann, 'if you think this is pungent!') One by one, people moved to the front of the coach, where, Mr McGann assured them, they'd feel better.

That's how it happened that Matt, having been sitting at the front on his own (not because he got travel sick, but because he had no friends) was soon in the middle of things and worried that even the empty seat beside him might be filled. He started rearranging his coat and his bag to be more spread out, and when he glanced up he found himself looking right into a face wedged between the two seats in front.

The face was Jazzy O'Hanlon's, and her big, brown eyes were watching him, laughing.

'That won't stop somebody sitting there,' she said.

'It might.'

'It won't.' And to prove it, she slipped out into the aisle and sat there herself. She plonked the coat and the bag on his lap and grinned. 'See?'

Jazzy and her family lived right next door to Matt and

his. When Matt had moved in, he'd worried about this: living next door to a girl in the same year at school. But Jazzy hadn't been a problem and he'd been able to keep himself to himself. Till now.

'Jazzy, where are you?' came Tash Lawes's voice. 'I need you! Where've you gone?'

Matt Barker was not a quick thinker. (At least, not unless he was playing football.) He wanted to say something stern, if not rude, to Jazzy O'Hanlon now, but all he came up with was, 'Your friend needs you. Didn't you hear?'

'Oh, Tash'll survive.' She waved a hand vaguely. 'Chocolate?' She offered him some.

'You shouldn't eat that,' said Matt. 'You should suck boiled sweets if you're feeling sick.'

'But I'm not!' she said triumphantly.

'Then why—'

Quick as a flash, she cut in. 'You have – got – something, haven't you?'

He couldn't think what she was talking about. Was it the empty seat next to him? Did she mean he had an infectious disease? No. Though he wished she'd leave him alone, he felt she wasn't being nasty.

'Yesterday,' she went on. 'What you said in the game. You *have* got – something – haven't you? At home?'

Unprepared for the question and surprised by her directness, he said, 'Yes.'

'What?'

But he wouldn't be caught out again. I don't have to answer, he told himself, we're not playing that stupid game any more.

If he'd listened to begin with, when Mr McGann had explained the rules, he'd have understood that he didn't *have* to say anything at all: that you only spoke up if you had a remarkable thing you *wanted* to share. He'd said what he'd said because he'd thought he must. Mr McGann had gone on about how the best stories were often true, and most people had one inside them, although they might not want to tell it, which was perfectly OK.

But Matt had been taking a penalty for England, in injury time, and missed that bit. After the shot (and over the roar of the crowd) he'd heard Mr McGann finish up,

'You must be prepared to answer questions,' and then, it seemed almost at once, it was his turn: 'So. Matt?'

All he knew was he must speak the truth and it must be something unusual. He wasn't a quick thinker. He had no choice.

'What did you *mean* about seeing a fairy?' Jazzy O'Hanlon said now. Her eyes were unbelievably big. 'What did you really see? What did you do? *What happened?*'

'Jazz, come *back*!' called Tasha, but Jazzy ignored her as before.

'Look!' he said, pointing. 'We're there!'

He'd never have thought you could be so pleased to see a field full of goats.

Nobody liked the cheese. When the dumpy woman who'd shown them round had advanced on them with handfuls of little wrapped balls to take home, they'd all backed away.

'Non, merci!'

Only Tasha had turned it into 'mercy' and raised her hands in mock surrender, which made them laugh.

Standing beside her, laughing as well, Jazzy smacked her lightly and said, 'Don't!', because the woman was looking confused. No one had laughed when she'd wanted them to: when she'd pointed at the baby goats and said, 'Keeds!' and then swivelled round and pointed at *them* and said it again.

'No one want cheese?' she said, disappointed, and Angela Poole stepped forward.

'I do. I like it,' she said. 'It's delicious.'

Then Mr McGann said something in French, and whatever it was made the woman smile and pack the cheeses for them in ice and insist they take them away.

'Pooh!' said Jazzy, beside him again as they drove back along the bendy road. 'This coach really stinks! Why did we have to take that lot with us? Nobody wants it!'

'Angela does.'

'Angela? Oh, she just said that. She doesn't really. Her parents are getting divorced.'

'Well, what's that got to do with it?' He felt cross.

Really he wanted to say, 'Why are you still sitting next

to me?' He didn't want this girl disturbing his thoughts with her constant chat. *Leave me alone.*

'Angela tries to be nice to people all the time, to make them feel good. *I* think it's better to be honest. That way, you don't get landed with a load of cheese!'

'Nothing wrong with doing things to be nice to people,' he said pointedly. 'You should give it a go.'

Jazzy looked at him in surprise. 'Are you trying to tell me something?'

'No. But, well, wouldn't you rather go back and sit with Tasha?'

'You're trying to tell me to go away!' She laughed merrily. 'But I don't want to! I want to sit here!'

'Why?'

'Because I like you, of course!'

He felt alarmed.

'Why?'

'You sound like my sister. Melissa. *She* always says, "Why?"' She adjusted her voice to sound like someone explaining something to a very young child. 'I like you because you're an in-tresting person.'

Matt was stunned. No one had *ever* said that. His mum called him one-track minded. He couldn't think what on earth to say next.

'That thing you said yesterday, in the game . . . '

'Oh, *that*!' he burst out. 'Wish I'd never said that!'

She ignored him. 'I'm interested in fairies.'

'I'm not,' he said rudely, hoping to crush her.

'Well, I am. Because I'm playing one.'

'What do you mean?'

'Ha! Now you know what it's like! When someone says something you don't understand.' She paused, deciding whether or not to explain. Matt hadn't explained yesterday. She could do the same back. But then they'd get nowhere. 'I'm playing a fairy in a Shakespeare play.'

'Shakespeare?' he was contemptuous. '*Shakespeare? What's he got to do with anything? What—*'

'A lot, if you want to know!' Jazzy said hotly. 'He's really relevant – now more than ever. He makes you *think*. He's brilliant!'

'He's dead,' said Matt.

Jazzy went quiet. 'You're – what an *ignorant* thing to say! Only a *totally ignorant* person could say that. Don't you know *anything*? Do you know *nothing* except about football?'

No one spoke for a moment. Then, 'How did you know?' said Matt.

'Know what?'

'About me and football.'

Jazzy said, 'Oh, I just do. Everyone does. Mikey, Dip, Joe. They were going to ask you to play yesterday, only then they weren't so sure, after . . . '

'How d'you mean?'

He knew about Mikey, Dip, Joe, the footballing boys, who Mr McGann said might as well all three be joined at the hip (only then they'd have trouble running about). Their names were certainly fused: Mikey, Dip, Joe. No one ever said 'and'.

'How d'you mean?' said Matt. 'About yesterday?'

'I mean after what you said in the Truth Game. They thought it was weird. I heard them talking.'

Matt suddenly punched the seat in front.

'Leave me alone!' he said, this time out loud. 'Just go away!'

But in less than twenty-four hours she was back.

They had spent the day at Mont Saint-Michel, which was a heap of rocks in the sea, with an old medieval abbey built on top. Jazzy and Tash and the rest had noisily counted the steps you had to climb, and lost count and argued and had a good laugh. As Tash's best friend, Jazzy got to do everything first (with Tash) and everyone else had to follow behind. Not that Jazzy was like that. But still, it was fun being first up Mont Saint-Michel.

The boys had gone up in their own little groups, some counting the steps, some not. Matt had gone up alone.

But on the coach, on the way back to the hostel, that face had popped up again in the gap between the two seats.

Jazzy beamed. 'Sorry about what I said. About football.'

She hadn't said anything much. But still. He grunted. 'What is it now?'

13

'I want to tell you about Ariel.'

'What?'

'Ariel. The fairy I play.'

He groaned.

'Not a fairy with wings and a wand. Not the pink kind. Shakespeare calls him a spirit. *You* could have said "spirit" instead of "fairy". Why didn't you? If you'd said "spirit", it would have been better for you, I think.'

Yes, why hadn't he? Stupid. She was tiresome, but she was right.

'Anyway, Ariel's locked in a tree—'

'A tree?' Matt interrupted.

Hearing his sudden interest, she paused, and he saw he'd revealed too much.

'How can you be locked in a tree?' he went on, quickly and scornfully. 'You get locked in a house, or a prison or a loo—'

'Yes! The tree is like Ariel's prison. A witch shut him in it—'

'A witch?'

'Yes, a witch, and along comes this magician—'

'*Magician?*'

'Yes – and lets him out.'

But Matt had had more than enough. 'What happens to him in the end? Does he die?'

'Ariel? No, of course not. Spirits – *fairies* – can't die!'

Then Matt said a very surprising thing, his second in three days.

'I think they can.'

Chapter 2

WHAT MATT BARKER SAW

He'd been walking Dash. Mum had said, 'Take her out one last time before you go to France.' He hated the way she'd said that, as if Dash might die while he was away. Dash was old, but not that old: twelve. That was eighty-four in dog years. Lots of people lived to well over a hundred. It was a fact. Those cards sent from Buckingham Palace on your hundredth birthday were pointless now, but they had to keep sending them, now they'd started. Imagine being the first *not* to get one. You'd feel really let down.

Dash was going to live loads more years. But he took

her out anyway. He took her to Burnham Mount, their favourite place.

One of Mum's favourite things to say was that Matt was away with the fairies. Meaning he was a dreamer – though it wasn't so much fairies as football, with him. She worried he lost concentration too easily. She worried (just ever so slightly) every time he took Dash for a walk.

'Don't forget you're *responsible* for her,' she said. 'Keep her close when you cross the road. And don't let her off till you're sure it's OK. Matt, are you listening? Don't let those fairies distract you! Remember, Dasher's safety is in your hands!'

She needn't have worried. At least, not about Dash's safety.

'Oh, and clear up if she does a poo! Matt?' He was already out of the door and she had to run after him, down the path, with a bag. 'Promise you'll clear up after her, Matt!'

He didn't promise, but he took the bag and shoved it deep in his trouser pocket. When Dash did a poo on the pavement, two minutes later, he kicked it skilfully into the grass.

Mum needn't have worried about Dasher's safety, though. Soon after they'd left the village, the pavement ran out and they had to walk on the road, but Matt kept the little dog close. Football wasn't the only thing he cared about – though it did take up most of his head space.

The track up Burnham Mount began with a gate and, beside it, a sign: 'Footpath to the Burnham Stone 1/4'. Burnham Stone was the village that Matt and his family had moved to; *the* Burnham Stone was a lump of rock which must once have been important enough to give the village its name. Those who knew why were long gone. But the Stone was still somewhere people went. Boyfriends and girlfriends, to hold hands at sunset; families, out for their weekend stroll. When little kids played tag up there, it was always 'Home'.

As soon as Matt was through the gate, he let Dash off the lead and she pottered ahead of him, shoving her nose into clumps of grass to discover who'd been there before. This was a hobby of hers, and she weed on each clump before moving on, to give the next dog (as Dad always liked to say) the same pleasure.

Matt clipped the lead round her neck and set off up the track.

It was a lovely, warm spring day. The fields on either side of the track had been planted with a crop that was just beginning to come up. The sun caught the delicate spikes of green, and the further away you looked, the more the spikes merged together, so that in the distance they became one pale green haze. You could see to the horizon, till the track took you into the wood.

Burnham Wood was not the sort you'd choose for a picnic. Not that it was unpleasant, but it was dense and prickly in a way that suggested you'd never have found a space clear enough to lay your picnic rug down. It had the appearance of somewhere private. There weren't any signs saying keep out, it was just that it didn't look inviting. It looked like a place that had secrets to keep. Dash always went in, but that was different.

Dash loved Burnham Wood even more than she loved the track leading up to and through it. Matt always kept to the track, but as soon as it entered the wood, Dash was gone. Matt didn't worry, he knew she was safe; they were far enough from the road. He didn't know what she got up to in there, but pheasants were often involved: you could hear their outraged squawks now and then, and the flap and fuss as they rose through the trees. Once there had been a sharper alarm – the call of a different bird, or a rodent – but Dash was too old to catch anything now, Matt knew. She just had fun.

Burnham Wood went round the shoulders of Burnham Mount like a cloak, or at least a wide scarf. The track took you straight up through it and then turned right and went up a bit more. So now you were in the top field (which the wood encircled), with the wood on your right. You could see to the top of the Mount now: there on the skyline was the Burnham Stone.

It wasn't large, for a landmark that had its own sign and was marked on the map: only about the size of a lying-down cow. Once it had been larger, but the farmer who had to plough round it all the time had at last lost patience and had the idea of smashing it up. He'd begun, but a crowd of people who lived in the village had come and stopped him, and now the Stone was protected by law, and all farmers after him had to plough round it – and sow their crops round it – and harvest around it, when the time came. (One of them, more recently, had applied for permission to plough up the *wood*. But the council had said no – the wood was an ancient feature of the landscape and a haven for wildlife; it must stay.)

When Matt reached the brow of the hill, he left the edge of the wood, as everyone did, and walked the last little bit of the way to the Stone through the field itself. The path at this point was no more than the crop trampled down by people's feet. These days, the farmer resigned himself to the irritation of it: he knew better than to try changing things, which only led to trouble. Matt, with his trainers white and chalky from the field, sat on the Stone as you might sit on a bench.

If ever he had any sweets with him when he came here, that's where he ate them, but he hadn't today. If he'd had any friends to text, that's where he'd text them, but all his friends were back at his old home, and texting them now would make him feel sad. Mum said he'd soon make new ones – on the trip to France, he was bound to. He hoped she was right. Sitting here on this rock, he felt bored and alone.

And then, from somewhere back in the wood, Dash barked.

The wood went right round this top field and she could have been anywhere in it. She sometimes went in really deep, but she hadn't today. He could tell by the sound. The surprising thing was that she'd made any sound at all: in general, she wasn't a barker. (That was Dad's great joke: we're all of us Barkers, except the dog!)

She barked again.

'Dash!' Matt called, and immediately wished he hadn't. If she came, he'd never find out what the big deal was. Her bark had sounded excited, and he could do with a bit of excitement right now. She didn't come, but barked once more, and this time he got up and hurried back through the field, towards the wood. He couldn't see any obvious way in, so began retracing his steps down the track, looking to his left all the time, for an opening. There were plenty of rabbit holes in among the roots of the thorn bushes edging the track, but nothing large enough to be useful to him.

He came to the point where the track turned off the field to cut through the wood, and he took the turn. If he didn't find an opening soon, he'd be out of the wood on the other side, and he'd have to give up and call Dash back and take her home. He took a kick at a toadstool in the grass and the head flew off to the left and landed on a patch of bare earth surrounding a cluster of three or four big rabbit holes. Something, perhaps a fox – perhaps Dash – had scrabbled away at them, making quite a sizeable excavation.

Could he crawl through?

And even if he could, *would* he? Did he really want to go into the wood, he asked himself? Nobody else did; they went to the Stone, which was friendly and safe.

But Matt was bored.

If he went right down on his belly, he could use the freshly made hollow to wriggle in under the thorns. What if he did? Would more thorns, further in, force him back?

So what? He'd get dirty – but Mum would be washing these clothes, anyway, while he was in France.

Dash barked. *Come on!*

Matt flung himself down and pressed himself flat to the earth and pushed himself forward.

It was horrid.

People who go exploring in caves or down potholes may like being shut in – but Matt, though he wasn't even under the ground, felt trapped, and nearly panicked. If he lifted his head, thorns jabbed at his scalp. If he stretched out an arm, they caught his sleeve. But he pushed on, and suddenly found he *could* lift his head without being jabbed. He was through the thorns.

He got to his knees, then his feet. Crouching, because he was still among branches, he stumbled forward. He was surprised to find that the wood wasn't all bushes and scrub, as he had supposed. In amongst the dense tangle were trees, proper trees, that you couldn't see from the track.

There was no sign of Dash, but leading into the wood was a kind of path, which he started to follow. It could only be used by woodland creatures – he kept having to stoop to avoid low branches – but it was better than nothing. And it led him to a clearing, into which sunlight slanted down through the boughs of a truly majestic tree on the further side. This tree spread itself overhead, a bit like the ceiling of a cathedral, but at its foot was a more homely sight.

Dash was there, with her front legs stretched out and her bottom stuck comically up in the air. You might have thought she'd seem out of place, but somehow she didn't. Her tail was wagging like mad and she was watching something intently, just up from the level of the ground. She couldn't take her eyes off it, couldn't afford to look round, but she knew Matt was there, he could tell, and she barked again. That same, excited bark. Playful, almost.

She looks like a puppy, Matt thought, and was glad he'd come, if for no other reason.

And then he saw what she was seeing.

He saw it for only two seconds, but they were to shape the whole of his summer and – who knows what influence things have on people? – maybe his life.

A largish branch had broken off from the tree and crashed to the ground. It lay there amid a confusion of smaller branches and snapped-off twigs. It was too early on in the year for leaves; there was just this tangle of twigs and sticks and, sticking up out of it, one twig in particular. This twig was quite short, quite straight and quite slender.

Unremarkable, you might say.

Except it was moving.

Matt shook his head. *Twigs move all the time*, he thought. *In the wind, or when somebody shakes the branch that they're attached to.*

But this twig was not attached to a branch. And besides, there was nobody there.

It didn't make sense.

The twig twisted and turned in mid-air, with a life of its own.

It must be a trick of the light.

But no.

It must be the wind.

But there was no wind.

It might have been spooky, but Matt had no time to be scared. Because, suddenly, as he watched, the life went out of the twig (if it was a twig) and – right there, right then – it died.

How could he know it had died, when he'd hardly known it had been alive? It suddenly writhed in the air, then went rigid and fell. And he just *did*.

And he cried out, 'No!' because nobody likes seeing something actually die. Whether it's Angela's grandpa – or this. He stuck his fists in his eyes and rubbed them.

Maybe he rubbed them too hard. Because straight after that, he saw something else.

Or thought he did.

He never told anyone else about it. He never saw it again, and dismissed it as just his imagination. It didn't seem connected to the twig.

A human figure it was, quite tall – though whether a man or a woman, he couldn't have said. A figure *going away*, though as far as Matt knew, it had never been there in the first place. Going away from him soundlessly.

Going where, impossibly, there was no path. And yet going – receding – quite fast. Getting smaller.

Disappearing into the trees.

The shock of seeing the twig must have messed with his brain.

Dash came over to greet him, wagging her tail, swishing it low, as she always did for people she knew. But Matt ignored her for once, and ran forward. He never doubted that he'd recognise what he was looking for in amongst all the debris of ordinary twigs on the ground. He picked it up without hesitation.

It felt like an ordinary twig, itself, as he held it, barely reaching across the span of his outstretched hand. It had little black buds pressed in close to the bark, he noticed: a pair, about halfway along, and a single one, bigger but no less black, at the end. These buds made him think of delicate paws or tiny, pointed hooves, but even they weren't extraordinary, the twigs on the ground had them, too.

What was strange was he could – just – also see what *his* twig had been before. It was two things at once. A twig and – what? He couldn't have given it a name, if someone had asked: but no one was going to, were they?

He put it in the plastic bag from his pocket, called Dash and turned back.

They left the wood the same way he'd come in. (There wasn't any other.) Dash seemed familiar with the path. When they came to the scooped-out passageway under the outer wall of thorns, she slipped through, no problem, with just some mud getting stuck to her fur. But Matt had even more trouble than before.

This time, he had his find to protect – and he couldn't put it in his pocket, in case it got broken. The thorns kept snagging the plastic bag – and the skin of his hand – so that when at last he emerged, the bag was torn and his hand was bleeding. But the hard, knobbly thing inside the bag was safe; he could feel it. He didn't know why he wanted to take it home, nor what he would do when he had. But he carried it carefully down the track as if it were as precious to him as the little black dog at his side.

Chapter 3

THE TRUTH GAME: REPLAY

Jazzy wasn't stupid, though some people thought she sort of was. It was the way she seemed to come out with things straight away, without any gap between what she felt and what she said. But she worked something out that nobody else did. Tash wasn't stupid, but she didn't get it. Not even Matt himself would have done: his intelligence was a different kind again.

What Jazzy worked out was two things: why Matt had said what he'd said in the Truth Game, and how to get him to say more.

*

'You shouldn't keep coming to sit here,' said Matt.

He couldn't think why she did. The seat beside his on the coach was never, ever empty now. She'd said she liked him, but that didn't really explain it. It wasn't that he didn't like her, but she wasn't the kind of friend he needed. In any case, she was a chatterbox and he didn't feel like chatting.

'It might start a rumour,' he said, knowing that girls cared about such things. There'd been one like Tash at his old school, who had caused no end of trouble. But he saw Jazzy wasn't impressed, and so finished lamely, as he'd begun: 'You shouldn't sit here.'

'Oh, nobody cares, on a trip!' she said brightly. 'On school trips, everything's different. Haven't you noticed? The rules have changed. People don't say what they'd normally say – or sometimes they *do* say what they wouldn't back home. That's what I like about trips. When you go back home, the rules change back, but on the trip, everything's – different.'

He wasn't surprised she liked acting. That wasn't chat, it was a speech! Shakespeare had a lot to answer for.

'The Truth Game always works best on a trip,' Jazzy added, casually.

They were on their way to have a look at the Bayeux Tapestry: 'the very first graphic novel', Mr McGann had grandly said. It would tell them the story of how the French had come over to England in 1066 and shot King Harold in the eye.

Matt felt as if *he* had been shot in the eye. He groaned, perhaps not so loudly as Harold, and wished for the end of the journey.

'The Truth Game is stupid,' he said. 'What's the point?'

'None, if you lie,' said Jazzy.

'I didn't!'

'I never said you did. But everyone *thinks* you did. Except me. Mr McGann does. Angela. Tash.'

'Let them!' he said, looking desperately out of the window.

'Mikey, Dip, Joe.'

'So? Who cares?'

'You do,' said Jazzy.

*

It turned out that Harold might not have been shot in the eye, after all.

'Oh, I hope he wasn't!' said Angela, with feeling.

'Well, *somebody* was,' said Joe.

'Not necessarily,' said their guide. 'The arrow we can see might have been added in later, for effect.'

'Well, anyway, he was killed,' said Thomas Dunn. Thomas had something wrong with his bladder, which meant he needed the toilet a lot. Right now, he obviously wanted to get this question sorted out quickly.

'He certainly was,' said the guide. He smiled. 'But it might not be Harold we're looking at!' Despite knowing everything, he hadn't worked out the thing about Thomas.

'But you said . . . Who *are* we looking at, then? It's *someone* dying.'

'Young man, *thousands* died at the Battle of Hastings! You might as well say—'

But at this point, Mr McGann interrupted. 'Thomas, come with me.' He raised his eyebrows at him. 'Now.'

*

33

In the gift shop, Matt spent all his money on a dustbin.

It wasn't a dustbin exactly – it didn't have a lid – but it was made of metal and about that size. Of course it was all clean and new and decorated with a large-scale reproduction of part of the Tapestry – the part showing Harold and the arrow (of course). You couldn't help feeling that it *must* be Harold because everything in the shop had him on. As soon as you walked in, you felt that the people who'd made the gifts ('Hardly gifts, at these prices!' said Mr McGann) must know something the guide did not.

Everyone else bought King Harold chocolate and King Harold notebooks and King Harold pens. The pens were made to look like the arrow, and each one was stuck in a holder made to look like King Harold's head. It caused quite a stir when Matt bought his bin, not only because it was such a strange choice, but also because the shop had been using it as a poster tube stand, and all the poster tubes had to be taken out and stood elsewhere.

'That's a big sick bucket,' Joe said to Matt, as they walked back out to the coach. 'Could be useful.'

'It's a waste-paper bin,' said Matt.

'That's a big waste-paper bin, then,' said Joe, to show he meant no harm.

But, on the coach, Matt still made for his usual seat at the front, far away from the others. Not *right* at the front, since that would have meant being too close to Spike and Mr McGann. The coach was much too big for their group; he could sit a few seats in and still distance himself from everyone else. Or so he hoped.

He sat his bin beside him and felt secure. When Jazzy's face appeared in the gap between the two seats in front, he looked at her and spread his palms and shrugged.

'Sorry,' he said, 'too big to go in the overhead rack.'

'Nice one,' said Jazzy.

He couldn't tell whether she meant the bin or his tactics. Her face disappeared and he felt triumphant. He glanced at the great shiny cylinder next to him and thought: *Money well spent*. But two seconds later, Jazzy was there, in the aisle, with her hands on the bin.

'Got it!' she said. 'Me and Harold swap places! He won't mind!' She made her voice deep and respectful:

'You won't mind, will you, Your Majesty? I mean, Your Royal Shot-in-the-eye-ness!'

There was a ridiculous moment during which she was lifting the bin by its top and Matt was trying to clasp it lower down. But, being able to grip the edge, she easily won, and Harold was whisked to the seat in front.

'How do *you* think he died?' she asked, when she'd settled herself and pulled out a bar of Battle of Hastings chocolate.

Matt was too affronted to look at her. 'No idea.'

She burst out laughing.

'No *eye*-dea! That's brilliant! Tash thinks it was the arrow, but I don't. Too neat. Dying in battle isn't like that. I know, from Shakespeare.'

'And he's always right, is he?' Matt said sarcastically.

Jazzy ignored him.

'Talking of Shakespeare,' she said, 'and dying, what happened to that fairy you saw? How come *it* died?'

Matt was totally caught by surprise. 'What d'you . . . ? How . . . ?'

'How do I know? Easy!' She laughed again. 'You told me!'

'I never!'

'Oh, yes, you did! Not in so many words, not straight out, but you said just enough. It began with the Truth Game.'

'That? I was making that up! I took it all back! Didn't you hear? Angela gave me a second chance, remember, by asking again?'

'But she didn't, did she?' said Jazzy. 'She asked the wrong question. She asked if you had a real, live fairy at home, and you said no. That was the truth. But what you said first, *that* was the truth, as well. It *was* alive – and then it wasn't. So . . . it must have died!'

Matt stared at her.

'When? When did it die? When you got it home? *How* did it die? Did you kill it?'

'No!'

'Did it suffocate on the way back, in the bag?'

'*No!*'

'What, then?'

Matt half-closed his eyes. He was too old to cry. If his new bin had been within reach, he'd have brought it down over his head, to shut Jazzy out. Her and her questions.

'It died right after I saw it.'

'Killed by the power of your gaze!'

'OF COURSE NOT! IT WAS NOTHING TO DO WITH ME! I JUST HAPPENED TO BE THERE!'

Mr McGann leaned out of his seat to peer up the aisle.

'Hey!' he said. 'Calm down, whoever's shouting! There's no need for that: plenty of room for everyone to have personal space on this coach!'

'There!' said Matt. 'You heard! You're in my personal space! Get out!'

But Jazzy went on as if nothing had happened. 'Where? *Where* did you "happen" to be?'

'I . . .' And then, to even his own surprise, quite suddenly, Matt gave up. Perhaps he sensed Jazzy wasn't going to. Perhaps it was as she had said: on a trip, the rules change. You could do things and say things in the knowledge that, when you got home, it would all be forgotten. But there was a third possibility. No, a fact. Matt Barker was lonely. Even though Jazzy was not his choice, she was, it seemed, a friend.

And so he told her.

He told her about Burnham Wood (well, she knew about that, everyone did) but he told her about *getting in* and she was impressed.

'Don't you know what's in Burnham Wood?'

'No?' He hadn't meant to make it sound like a question.

'Ghosts! You can ask anyone: Burnham Wood's haunted!'

'Kids' stuff!' he scoffed. 'That's rubbish. That's not how it is.'

And he told her about the path and the clearing and Dasher and the tree.

At last he described what he'd seen underneath it. (The thing he'd seen after had gone from his mind.)

'It was Mum's fault I called it a fairy. She always says . . . It wasn't like how you'd imagine a fairy at all.'

'But it definitely wasn't a ghost?'

'No.'

(Nor was the other thing, either, but forget that for now.)

'Sometimes,' said Jazzy, 'the things that pop into your head are right. I'm *glad* you said "fairy". To call a twig a fairy makes everything even more bizarre. If you know what I mean?'

'You believe me, then?' Now he'd told her, he really wanted her to.

'Of course! You were playing the Truth Game, weren't you? Then and now.'

He hadn't realised this was the Truth Game again, but didn't try to argue. In a way, she was right.

'What kind of bag did you put the fairy in, to take it home?'

'A poo bag.'

'Eurghh!'

'It was clean! I hadn't used it. Mum always makes me take one when I take Dash for a walk, just in case.'

'I've seen you, coming out of your house.'

This wasn't surprising, but it unsettled Matt to think he'd been watched from next door.

Oblivious to his unease, though, Jazzy went on: 'Dash is cute. Why's she called that? Is that what she does?'

'Yes, and we got her at Christmas time. One of Santa's reindeers is . . .'

'Dasher!' said Jazzy triumphantly. 'My auntie's dog is called Soot. He's black as well, but he's not going grey. Is Dash old?'

'No!'

He'd have said – and believed – this was still in the Game. One person's truth can be different from another's. But suddenly he'd had enough.

When Jazzy asked where the fairy was now, he pretended not to hear.

And when she said could she come round and see it, when they got back home tomorrow, he said no.

On the other side of the English Channel (or 'la Manche', if you're in France), on the edge of the village of Burnham Stone, in a house with a 'Sold' sign still posted outside, there was at this moment a heartfelt cry. Matt's mum, tidying his bedroom, had caught sight of a poo bag and reached for it and discovered it wasn't empty.

How could he? she thought. How *could* he? When would he learn some common sense? She'd always laughed that his room was unhygienic, but this was beyond a joke.

She overcame her disgust and picked up the scrunched bag, with finger and thumb. It wasn't smelly, thank goodness: at least he must have tied the top.

She quickly took the thing outside and threw it away.

Chapter 4

HOMECOMING

All the girls hugged their mums and dads when they got off the coach. Then they hugged each other.

'Jazz, don't leave me!' wailed Tash, and pretended to cry.

But Jazzy's whole family had come, and she had to hug *them*, again and again – her mum, her dad, her big brother, Nige, and Melissa. Melissa bobbed up and down, bending her knees as if trying to take off.

'Jazzy!' she kept saying. 'Jazzy! Lovely Jazzy! Oh, *please*!'

That meant '*pick me up*', and although she was really too big to be picked up now, Jazzy did.

Some of the boys let themselves be hugged, but most

didn't. Matt's mum and dad knew what he was like, and only his dad had come.

'Good time?' he said, patting his son on the shoulder.

'Yeah.'

'Everything's OK at home. Your mum. Luke.'

'Dash?' said Matt.

But Dad didn't hear. He was putting Matt's stuff in the boot.

'Nice bin,' he said. 'Your mum'll be pleased. She spring-cleaned your room while you were away. She could have done with a whopping great bin! Still, better late than never.'

Matt might have worried at this news, if he hadn't been worrying about something else. He couldn't ask again.

'In other news,' said Dad as he started the car and switched on the headlights, 'your mother and I went round for coffee with the O'Hanlons.'

He waited for Matt to say something, but Matt didn't. So he added, 'The people next door?'

Matt said, 'I know.'

'They're friendly enough, but she's a painter. Rosie or

Daisy or something. No, Poppy. She's painted their lounge to look like a beach. With kids in the sea and an ice-cream seller and donkeys.' He paused, remembering, shaking his head. 'I saw them just now, in the playground.'

'The donkeys?'

'No! The O'Hanlons. Their elder daughter was on the trip. Did you know? She's a bit of an actor, it seems. Did you talk?' He lowered his voice. 'The mum's a bit mad. What's this actor daughter like?'

'Same,' said Matt.

The conversation had never been lively, and, as they were almost home, Dad let it die.

But Matt's fears for Dash were unfounded. When the two of them walked through the door, she flung herself at him, with yelps of joy. He dropped his bag and sat on the stairs and held her while she wriggled and squirmed in his arms. What she wanted to do most of all was press her muzzle against his face.

'Dash,' he kept saying. 'Dash. Dash. It's all right.' But her whining made it sound as if she were in pain.

'*Somebody's* glad to have you back!' said Mum,

coming into the hall. 'Luke!' she shouted. 'Matt's home!' But she got no response. Luke would be in his room, with his headphones on.

Dash was quieter now, so Matt put her down and started upstairs.

'Bag!' his mum shouted. 'Take it with you!'

But he had gone.

She directed a questioning glance at his dad, who was standing, holding the bin, but Dad misinterpreted the look.

'Souvenir!' he said. 'Here, you have a go – it's great!' He shoved it at her. 'I'm going to put the kettle on!'

She wasn't surprised by the bin. Its oddness was typical of Matt. It would have been much more surprising if he'd brought home a tea towel or a nice box of chocs. But she did wonder at his keenness to rush upstairs. *Why the hurry?* she said to herself. It wouldn't be to see Luke: she heard him bang on Luke's door with the flat of his hand as he went down the passage. 'Go away!' yelled Luke, unnecessarily loud. Maybe he wanted to see his room. She'd asked his dad to prepare him for what she'd done, but couldn't be sure if he had.

'Did you tell him?' she called towards the kitchen, but quietly, so Matt wouldn't hear from upstairs. 'Did you tell him about me having a clear-out?'

The clear-out had taken her hours, but she didn't expect thanks. She didn't expect much reaction at all. Perhaps she'd misjudged him. She felt suddenly nervous. She heard him open his door, and close it behind him.

Deborah Barker put the bin down and shunted the bag beside it, against the wall, so neither would be a trip hazard, at least. In the kitchen, the kettle started boiling, and then two more sounds, at just the same time, drowned it out. They had nothing to do with each other, the cry from upstairs and the doorbell being rung, but they confused Deb, and she stood undecided which to attend to. The cry was anguished – angry, even. (So she *had* misjudged him. She braced herself.) The bell was insistent and sustained.

She stood like that in the hall, and Dash sat beside her with one paw lifted, hoping she'd choose to answer the bell. Dash loved visitors almost as much as pheasants and rabbits.

Suddenly, upstairs, a door burst open and Matt came hurtling down. He wasn't coming down to open the door, but there it was, in front of him – and the bell was still ringing – so he did. He opened it wildly and stood looking out at the person who was there. Dash danced round in delight.

'We've locked ourselves out,' Jazzy said quickly. 'That's why I've come. My mum gave your mum a spare key for safekeeping. Can we have it?'

He stared at her blankly, not hearing the words.

'It's gone!' he said.

Jazzy laughed. 'No! I don't believe it! You've lost it? Really? That's *funny*!'

She was trying to stroke Dash, but pulling her hand back as well because Dash had wrinkled her lips and her teeth were showing. People thought she was snarling when she did that, but she wasn't: it was just how she smiled.

'Jazzy! Jazzy!' came a high, sing-song voice from the darkness outside. 'Hurry *up*!'

And then Deb stepped forward and spoke to Jazzy over Matt's head. 'What nonsense! Of *course* we've not lost it!

Matt, what's the matter with you? I'll get it. Hang on.'

But when she came back with the key, Jazzy hadn't hung on. She had gone. So had Matt, so had Dash. Instead, a stout little girl was standing on the doorstep, apparently uncertain whether to come in. She was peering curiously up the stairs.

'Melissa, isn't it?' said Deb.

'Yes.'

These houses were newly built, and not really right for a smallish village. They belonged in a town. They had black painted railings in front and three stone steps each, leading up to the door. The steps and the railings made you think they were grand, but actually they were rather squashed together. Melissa hadn't had to come far by herself, and as she stood at the top of the Barkers' steps, she was almost within touching distance of the O'Hanlons'.

'Can you hold this really tight –' Deb put the key in the little girl's hand – 'and run back to your mum and give it to her?' She could hear the parents shuffling about as they waited outside their locked door. If she'd stuck out her head, she could even have said hello.

Melissa's fingers closed on the key, and went white. She watched this with interest. Then, with her face all screwed up to show how tightly she was squeezing, she looked at Deb for approval.

'That's right,' said Deb. 'Off you go!'

Jazzy sat on the edge of Matt's bed with Dash in her lap and a football player smiling down from a shiny poster above her head. She fondled the dog's soft ears – Dash and the footballer both looked pleased with themselves – and surveyed the immaculate room.

She was surprised. Her room wasn't bad, but it wasn't a patch on this – and she was a girl. Nige kept his room in a terrible state and all her friends who had brothers said the same: their rooms were like tips. Jazzy would never have had Matt down as a *tidy* person.

'What d'you mean, it's gone?' she said. She didn't need to ask what 'it' was, now. 'D'you mean it's escaped?'

'No! How could it? You don't understand!'

He didn't want her here. Once again, she'd forced her way in.

'But it's *magic*.'

'No.' Matt sat on the bed beside her and was stubborn. 'It's dead.'

'Then somebody must have taken it. I know! Dash!'

'No, she wasn't interested after it died. I saw. And anyway –' he looked severely down at Dash, who had quivered uncertainly at her name – 'she isn't allowed to come upstairs.'

Jazzy made a show of protecting Dash by grabbing a handful of duvet and wrapping her in it so only her head poked out. Dash went dreamy. She was in heaven.

'*I* know!' said Jazzy. 'Its family! Its friends! They came for its body! They wanted to bury it. You know – lay it to rest! You stole it from Burnham Wood and they wanted it back!'

This was a new one on Matt: that there might be others. You needed six people to carry a coffin, so perhaps six fairies . . . But the thought of a funeral was stupid. If his fairy had friends, they wouldn't make a coffin. Apart from anything else (and there were so many reasons why not), they didn't have hands.

Jazzy, for her part, was thinking of ants. She'd seen a film of hundreds of ants demonstrating teamwork and carrying things. She imagined a team of fairies from Burnham Wood swarming up the wall of Matt's house. They'd look like a vertical river, a rippling shadow, searching, seeking.

'How could they get in?' she said. 'Do you think your mum might have left a window open? You know, to air the room, while you were away?'

'She did more than that!' said Matt, shaking his head to clear it of nonsense. That was the trouble with Jazzy (one of the many): she got you going and swept you along. 'I'll tell you exactly what Mum did . . .'

He stopped, in despair.

'Yes?'

'Look under the bed.'

Jazzy moved Dash, all wrapped up in the duvet, off her lap, and knelt on the floor to peer under the bed. 'I can't see a thing. There's nothing there!'

'Exactly. She cleaned under there. She tidied. She *never* tidies under my bed. That's why I put it there, in amongst everything else, where it would be safe. She's always said she wouldn't dare go under there without wearing protective clothing. But she did.'

He jumped up and kicked the bed, hard – then clutched his toe. In pain and rage, he yelled, 'MUM!'

That's it, then, thought Deb, downstairs. She had transformed his room from a rubbish heap into a civilised living space, and she was going to be punished for it. She'd tried to make his homecoming happy. She'd even resolved not to lecture him on the disposal of dog poo bags – not be hard on him, as soon as he walked in. But these days it seemed she could get nothing right. She sighed and went into the hall.

And then, for the second time in fifteen minutes, a cry inside the house coincided with someone outside, on the bell. Matt bellowed again – and the doorbell went – and his mum had a reason to put off going upstairs.

Deb eyed the person on the doorstep. It was the mother, Poppy O'Hanlon, dressed in her funny, arty clothes.

She held out the spare key. 'Thanks for this. Would you mind hanging on to it, though? We're always locking ourselves out! Anyway, all in now – except now we've lost Jazzy!'

Just for a moment, Deb thought this strange woman had come to collect a spare child! They'd been given a spare *key* for safekeeping, so why not?

'Sorry,' she said, 'I haven't . . . '

'Oh, she must be here. She came to collect the key, but she never came back. Melissa said she'd gone.'

What a family! Deb thought. *Trust us to move in next door to a madhouse!* And then a voice called down from upstairs: not the angry one of a moment ago, but a cheerful one, a girl's.

'Coming, Mum!'

Jazzy appeared. She was cradling something wrapped in a duvet.

'Hurry up, then – we want you home! We've missed you! You can't come back from France and then go wandering off straight away!'

'Me and Matt had some things to discuss from the

trip.' Jazzy turned and called over her shoulder: 'Don't worry, I know what to do! Tell you tomorrow!'

She handed the bundle of duvet (with Dash looking anxiously out) to Deb.

Poppy O'Hanlon raised an eyebrow and winked. Deb felt bemused. She rubbed Dasher's head with her chin and found she couldn't even feel cross with Matt for having had her upstairs.

She wanted to say, *But this isn't right. All he's interested in is football. Not France. Not girls.* She smiled weakly as she closed the door behind Poppy and her daughter.

All he's interested in is football. She put Dasher gently down on the floor. *And you.*

Football and Dasher. Dasher and football.

Not bright, bubbly Jazzy O'Hanlon.

Chapter 5

DISGUSTING

They were all playing a game. That's what Jazzy had said or, at least, what he took her to mean. The game had rules, but not like in football.

He was starting to think he'd never play football again.

Jazzy had said, on a trip, the rules changed, the game became different, and after the trip it all went back to how it was before.

But it hasn't, thought Matt, *gone back*. He felt cheated. He suddenly saw Jazzy's game as one of those puzzles with silver balls. Each ball has a little round hole to sit in, and you shake them up, so they're rolling round freely, then try to get them to go back. And eventually they do. But how do you know they've all gone back to exactly the holes they were in before? You don't!

Jazzy would never have called round before, but now she did. (A big difference.) She came round again, the day after they'd come home, and sat beside Matt on his bed and explained her idea. It didn't take long.

'Is that it?' said Matt. He was deeply disappointed. He hadn't intended to carry on talking to Jazzy when they got back. He had told her, 'No, you can't come round.' But then, when she came for the key, she had taken advantage. He'd been in a state of shock and she'd seized her chance. And when she'd said she knew what to do to recover what was lost, he felt better. Perhaps it would turn out to be a good thing to have her along, after all. But no.

'Look for it?' he repeated in disbelief.

'Sometimes simple ideas are the best.' Jazzy sounded defiant. 'Better than nothing, anyway. What were *you* going to do? Have a row with your mum? And then what? That's clever!'

He'd had the row with his mum. It had got him nowhere.

He hadn't been willing to go into detail, so when Mum had asked if there was something specific she'd moved, he had blustered, no, she just shouldn't have touched *anything*, it was *his* room and didn't he have a right to be private?

That had set her off. Yes, he did, but not when it put his health at risk. The things she had found in that room . . . Did he realize? She'd actually had to dispose of . . .

But Matt had walked out.

And now he felt he was going to have another row – with Jazzy. Tell her to leave. Tell her not to come back.

And what then?

It was Saturday morning. His heart ached. On Saturday morning there was only one thing to do – and he couldn't. Back home, they'd already replaced him, and here he hung back. What he wanted most in the world was to join them – Mikey, Dip, Joe, the footballing boys – but how could he? He'd spoiled things. They thought he was weird.

He'd wanted a judgement from them, but not this. He'd wanted to prove himself, once and for all, on the pitch – but they'd judged him on something else, and now it was all too late. He may as well give himself up to looking for fairies, like Jazzy had said.

And what if he found one – *his* fairy – what then? It was dead and no use to him now. He'd spoiled things for nothing. How stupid was that!

And that's when he saw the connection – just when there seemed to be no hope left. Maybe his fairy could help put things right – the things it had messed up before? What if he found it and showed it to everyone else? It would be proof! They'd see what it *had* been – before it died – and believe him. They'd see that Matt Barker wasn't weird, after all.

He imagined standing in front of a crowd big enough to fill Wembley Stadium, holding it up for them all to see. And if Mikey, Dip, Joe were there, too . . . ?

'Look for it,' Jazzy had said.

She was right. And not just because there was nothing else now. Looking for it was *important*.

Jazzy said his mum would have thrown it away in the green wheelie bin. Whatever it was exactly – whatever she'd thought it was – it was clearly organic. So they dragged the green bin out of sight, behind the shed, and upended it on the grass. The good news was it hadn't been emptied for several weeks. The bad news was this meant it stank.

If Matt's mum thought his bedroom had been disgusting, she didn't know what disgusting was. When the stuff from the bottom of the bin came splopping out in great, oozing dollops, he nearly threw up. He felt his stomach convulse. He turned away and bent double and retched, like he had when the Crickleton striker had kneed him right where it hurt, last year.

'If you can't stand the heat, get out of the kitchen!' Jazzy mocked. She was either incredibly tough or she had no sense of smell.

He stayed bent over and tried not to breathe through his nose. 'Don't tell me! Shakespeare?'

'Nope! Just me, saying don't be pathetic! Come on, let's—'

She stopped. Still bent over, he couldn't see why. But it gave him a rare chance to get a word in. 'I'm not!'

She shut him up with an urgent whisper. 'Shh! Never mind! Matt, there's someone else here. *We're being watched!*'

They'd wanted to do this in private. They'd dragged the bin here so no one would see. Who could it be? Mum? Dad? Not Luke: he rarely emerged from his room these days, except to eat. Maybe Jazzy's mum, come to fetch her back as she'd fetched her last night.

But the tone of Jazzy's voice made it sound like someone more important than any of these.

Surely not the fairy itself, come alive? That would be *too* amazing.

He turned and looked.

It wasn't the fairy. It was someone who'd come round the side of the shed.

This someone was observing them with interest.

This someone was sniffing the air, but not with disgust; coming quickly – eagerly – forward.

He rounded on Jazzy. 'You . . . !'

Because it was Dash.

Jazzy was laughing. 'Well, who did you think it was? Your fairy? Come all the way back from fairyland, to help?'

'No! *Of course not!*'

At every turn, she made him feel stupid. She was too quick. He'd had it with her.

And then they both heard a small sound at their feet.

A small *lapping* sound.

'*Dash! NO!*'

He wanted to throw up all over again.

'Why do they *do* that?' shrieked Jazzy, laughing and horrified at the same time. 'Soot, you know, my auntie's dog, he does it, too. Once I even saw him eat his own . . .'

Matt shooed Dash away, back round the shed. As he passed the door, he popped in, and when he came out, he was carrying a garden fork and a trowel.

'Here,' he said, giving Jazzy the fork. 'Let's get going.'

They poked about in the mess. Some bits were practically liquid, others could still be identified: bread crusts, a chicken carcass, a lot of strange, grey-blue, mashed potato that had started to grow hair.

Jazzy kept saying, 'Oh my God! Oh my God!' The stench was something else.

And when we find it? thought Matt. *What then?* Would a dead fairy smelling of *this* be worth having? Worth what they were going through now? He was changing his mind about its importance.

He prodded the end of something sticking out of a mass of vegetable peel, but it was a blackened carrot. Best to give up.

To punish himself for having been stupid enough to start in the first place, he smacked his trowel down, flat, in a big dob of something brown and mushy. Brown juice splattered over his face and he started spitting because a drop had flown into his mouth. Jazzy looked up.

'What are you . . . ?' Her voice trailed away. Then she used her dramatic whisper again. 'Matt! We *are* being watched!'

He couldn't believe she would use the same trick twice. Did she think he was brain-dead? It was insulting. He scooped up some of the brown stuff and threw it at her. It hit her cheek and ran down her neck. He threw some more, which stuck in her hair.

Surprisingly, Jazzy did nothing. She didn't respond at all. She just stared.

But behind him, someone said, '*Gross!*'

He turned.

Standing by the shed, her face contorted in mixed disgust and amusement, was Tash.

Tasha was tall and slim and had long, blonde hair, which she liked to toss to express herself when words weren't enough. She tossed it now.

'I've been texting you, Jazz,' she said. 'Then I went round your house. Your mum said you were here. I wanted to ask if you felt like going into town, but . . . Eurghh! What are you *doing*?'

They both looked at her without speaking, their faces splattered and daubed with muck.

'God, Jazz!' she said. And then again, '*God!*'

And then it happened.

She raised her hand, the hand that was holding her phone and – *click!* – she had taken a picture.

Jazzy began to speak then, a little too fast.

'We're looking for something. Something's been lost. We think it may have been thrown in here.'

'*May* have been?' Tash said. 'You'd want to be sure, before going through that lot! Unless you *like* that sort of thing . . .'

She slipped her phone safely into her bag. 'I'll leave you to it, then. Have fun!'

'No, wait, Tash!' said Jazzy. 'I can explain!'

'Don't bother,' said Tash. 'I'll go into town with Kezzia. You carry on.'

She tossed her hair again and turned on her heel and disappeared back round the shed. They heard her say, 'Hello, dog,' halfway up the garden.

When she had gone, even Jazzy was despondent.

'She's right.'

(*Girls always are*, thought Matt.)

'We should have made sure.'

She acted as if it was that and nothing else that was making her gloomy.

'I'm going to talk to your mum – if you won't. I'm guessing you won't – or will you?'

Matt shook his head. He didn't want to talk, not to his mum, not to anyone.

And neither of them wanted to even think about Tash.

Neither mentioned the photo.

Chapter 6

JUST A STICK

When Jazzy went into the house to look for Matt's mum, the first person she saw was a tall, thin boy with headphones on, doing something in the kitchen. He was standing with his back to her. She could hear little sounds coming out of the headphones, so wasn't surprised to get no answer when she said, 'Hello?'

Luke had recently had his hair cut very short. At school, it made him look tough. But now, standing close behind him, she could see it was *so* short in places that the skin of his scalp showed through, soft and pink. She paused for a moment, just looking, before she moved round where he could see her.

'Yeah, yeah,' he said straight away, as if she had spoken, although she hadn't. It was as if she had said, 'Hurry up!' or 'Don't leave a mess!' or 'Shouldn't you be doing your homework?' Perhaps these were things he was used to hearing. But Jazzy had said nothing.

It turned out he was making himself a snack: a tower of cheese, ham and pickle, gherkins and crisps, mayonnaise and a number of things she couldn't quite see. The slices of bread, top and bottom, were a giveaway, though, and she said without hesitation, 'Great sandwich.'

'Yeah, yeah.'

He wasn't a craftsman. The board from which his creation rose was littered with blobs, splats and offcuts, and the structure itself looked untidy and unstable. But he finished it off with an unexpected flourish – he skewered the top with a cocktail stick – and Jazzy could see he felt pleased.

'What's that for?' she said, speaking extra loud, in the hope of prompting a different response.

He lifted a headphone away from one ear – Jazzy noticed, in doing so, he smeared it with jam – and said, 'What?'

She repeated her question.

'Oh, it's just a stick,' he said, 'to hold it together.'

She laughed. 'That won't hold it together! It only reaches a tiny way down!'

He looked annoyed. 'It's something I do.' Then: 'D'you want Matt? He's upstairs.'

'I don't and he isn't!' she returned. 'I'm after your mum . . .'

Luke looked at her then, and she thought he might actually say something helpful, but no. Then she thought he might make a remark about the mess in her hair, but he didn't do that, either. (What with that and the jam on his headphones, they looked a right pair.)

'What's that *smell*?' he said, making a face.

'It's Dasher. She found something in the garden.'

From her basket, Dash raised her head.

'Jesus!'

'D'you know where your mum is?'

'Upstairs.'

She wasn't, of course. (It was like there was something wrong with him, Jazzy thought briefly, but knew there wasn't. Nige said he did no work but knew more than the rest of them put together and would probably do amazingly in his exams.)

Deborah and Malcolm Barker were in the utility room (which was also the loo), kneeling down in front of the washing machine.

'Look! It's all gunged up!' said Deborah, waving a cloth soiled with muddy black grease. 'That's the problem!'

'It certainly stinks!' said Malcolm. 'It smells of rotting vegetables. God!'

He suddenly noticed Jazzy in the doorway.

'Hello!'

Jazzy was glad of the washing machine problem, since the smell could no longer be blamed on Dash, in her basket in the kitchen.

'You can buy stuff to get rid of that,' she said. 'We do.'

'There you go, Deb, we don't need a plumber!'

They both stood up, looking relieved.

'Did your friend find you in the garden?' asked Deborah. 'Natasha? She didn't stay long.'

'Yes, thanks. She was going into town, but Matt and me were too busy – I couldn't go with her. Actually, that's why I came in, to ask . . . Well, not about that, but about Matt's room . . .' She saw his mum stiffen. 'He really likes it, now he's got used to it –' Deborah made a noise in her throat – 'but we wondered if you remembered finding a bag – sort of, well, like a dog poo bag . . .'

'A poo bag? That bag was what started it all! When I spotted that bag, I realized enough was enough. The room was *insanitary* . . .'

'Yes, yes, I know – you were totally right. You had to throw the bag away. So you did. You threw it away in the bin. In the green bin. Correct?'

Deborah eyed this strange girl. Strange girl, strange mother, strange family. Even the littlest one had that confidence: you wouldn't have called any of them shy! Standing in front of her, pointing a finger, Jazzy was like a detective inspector, investigating a crime. But Deborah Barker had done nothing wrong. She resented the implication.

'No!' she said. 'No, not correct, actually. On this occasion –' she guessed there weren't many – 'you're mistaken.'

'But you threw it away?' Jazzy insisted. She wasn't feeling as confident as she looked. She hadn't intended to antagonize Matt's mum.

'Yes, I threw it away. Of course.'

'And as it was organic, you must have thrown it in the green bin!'

'What was *inside* was organic –' Deborah Barker couldn't believe they were having this discussion – 'but those bags are non-recyclable, and I wasn't about to open it, so I got rid of the whole thing, all in one go.'

'Chucked it over the hedge?'

'No! Of course not! I put it in the *black* bin.'

'Oh!' Jazzy struck her forehead with her palm, meaning, *Why didn't I think of that?* 'Makes perfect sense. Silly me. Thanks, Deb!'

Then she was gone.

The Barkers were silent for a moment.

'We should have asked for the name of the washing machine stuff,' said Malcolm.

'You go and knock on their door, if you like,' said Deborah. 'I'm not going. I need to lie down!'

There were only three things in the black bin, when they looked: an iron that had given up the ghost ('Give up the ghost, *that's* Shakespeare!' said Jazzy), a doormat that Dasher had chewed and a pale green poo bag, tied at the top. At first they couldn't see the bag, but Jazzy leaned in and shifted the mat, and there it was. They hooked it out with the garden fork, and now it was in Matt's hands.

He hesitated, suddenly nervous.

The thing in the bag was responsible for so much, and not just what had happened to his room. It had caused him to make a fool of himself on the coach, that day in France. It had brought him a load of grief. It had brought him Jazzy, ringing the bell all the time.

And now Tasha had come, with her phone, and who knew *what* would happen?

Could the thing in the bag really make things better? His hope that it might get him back into football seemed silly. He had a terrible feeling that his life was about to get worse.

But Jazzy was looking excited. 'Go on, then! Let's see!'

'It might not be exactly—'

'Go *on*!'

He untied the handles. 'You know—'

'Take it out!'

So he did.

He picked it out carefully, gently. There were the tiny black buds, like paws. He tried to imagine he was holding a mouse: anything other than what he most feared.

But it was no good.

Jazzy stared, then burst out laughing. She laughed so hard that she actually snorted, and in between snorts she managed to gasp the words, *'It's just a stick!'*

Chapter 7

NEVER GO BACK

So Jazzy would never come back. That was clear.

She'd believed in his fairy and now it was just an ordinary bit of wood. Dasher had known all along. If he'd had her sense, this would never have happened. Dash had known straight away that when the fairy died, it had *gone*. But Matt was not a quick thinker. (Yes, yes, except on the football field – but that wasn't relevant any more, was it?) And now he almost doubted himself. Had there ever been anything there at all?

But again he thought of Dasher: she'd seen it, smelled it – or something – before. Dash had known it had been there *then*, as much as she knew it had gone when it died. He had wanted to prove to Jazzy – and then the others

– he hadn't lied. It would have been easy! But his dream of producing the evidence *was* just a dream. Pretty much from the start, all the evidence he had had was no more than a stick.

He made himself throw it away – though not in the wheelie bin again. He dropped it in his King Harold bin, still splendid and unused.

Jazzy had said she believed him right from the start, but now she'd laughed. Now she'd never come back. He'd be back to square one: all alone again.

There was a second reason, too, why he knew she'd not come back.

The reason was Facebook.

On Tasha's timeline, there was a photo. The two of them, side by side, looking into the camera, their faces smeared with muck from the bin. And Tasha had written a caption for it: 'Jazzy & Matt like it dirty!!!'

Something woke Jazzy O'Hanlon in the middle of the night.

She'd had enough trouble getting to sleep in the first

place. She'd tossed and turned, going over and over it – what Tash had done.

She'd been Tasha Lawes's best friend for too long to remember what it felt like being anything else. But not for so long that she didn't remember who'd been it before: Lucy Rose.

Lucy was more a gazelle than a girl: delicate-looking, with long, slender legs and soft features and dark, sweeping lashes. She still hung round Tash, but now she was just the same as everyone else.

When Lucy and Tash had their big falling-out, nobody – least of all Lucy herself – understood what it was about. Tash was holding a beauty contest (everyone had to vote for the winner) but after Tash turned on Lucy like that, Lucy was too distressed to attend. Instead, she handed her piece of paper to Jazzy, to put in the box: 'I vote for Tash.' Everyone voted for Tash – Jazzy did – although everyone knew the most beautiful girl in their year was Lucy Rose.

Tash always made sure she got what she wanted. Whatever it took.

The night Tash uploaded the photo on Facebook, Jazzy

lay awake and remembered that time. Lucy Rose had accepted her fate in a way Jazzy wouldn't accept her own. She closed her eyes tight against the vision of the photo and the caption. She burrowed down under her duvet, rejecting their message. But it was hard. The more she tried falling asleep, the more she was roused by a sickening sensation of another kind of falling.

Falling out of favour.

She must have slept in the end, though, because in the middle of the night, something woke her up. The moon was shining, she could tell by the light coming in through her curtains, but that wasn't it. There had been a sound.

A voice. Someone calling. Two people. Calling a name.

And then she knew this was a dream. She'd got Tash on the brain: it was only natural she'd dream there were voices calling *her*.

'Tasha! Tash!'

The voices were desperate-sounding. Which, of course, they would be. Being desperate herself, it was only natural she'd dream desperate dreams.

'*Tash!*'

But then she recognized one of the voices.

Matt.

Which didn't make sense. Why would Matt be out there calling Tash? Why should Matt be calling someone he didn't even like – as if his heart would break – at one in the morning?

She pulled the pillow down over her head. Why should she care? She had done with Matt! (He'd been right; she would never go back to him now.) What with that stupid stick and the Facebook post, she knew what to do – she wasn't an idiot. Go back to Tash.

But when Jazzy heard Matt's voice – and the upset in it – she sat up in bed. This was no dream. She strained to listen more carefully and discovered she'd made a mistake about something else, too.

He wasn't calling Tash.

He was calling *Dash*.

There were two bad reasons why Jazzy could have done what she did next. The first was she couldn't resist drama. (At school, it was her best subject and what she was known for.) The second was the other voice: Luke's.

It called less often, though not without feeling. And Luke intrigued her.

But these were selfish reasons, and Jazzy was not a selfish person. What got her scrambling into her clothes was the thought of a friend in need.

Everyone, even Nige, was in bed when she opened her bedroom door. No light showed under anyone else's as she tiptoed on to the landing. The landing was a jungle: their mum had painted it with leaves. But except for the friendly giraffe that looked out from behind a bunch of bananas, there was nobody there. The giraffe smiled down on Jazzy as she crept towards the top of the stairs. And when she got to the bottom, it was smiling still, as much as to say it would keep her secret.

She let herself stealthily out of the house, leaving the door on the latch behind her.

The night was so light, things cast shadows: pale, cold shadows, which spiked the moonlight, just as those voices had spiked the silence and woken her up. Only now they'd stopped. Could the crisis be over?

Jazzy went down their three front steps and round the

railings and up Matt's front path. She climbed *his* three steps and stood outside his front door, wondering what to do. And suddenly the door opened, and there was Matt himself, looking wild, in his pyjamas. He seemed unable to take her in. He opened his mouth, but not to say hello.

'*Da-sher!*'

'You've lost her?' said Jazzy.

'She's gone! Mum and Dad always let her out just before they go to bed. She wees in the garden, then comes back in. But tonight she didn't. There's a hole in the fence . . .'

'I'll help you,' said Jazzy. 'I know what to do!'

Matt had heard this before. 'We *are* looking for her! What d'you think we're doing? Mum's driving round in the car. Luke's gone into the village.'

'No, no, I mean I know *where to look*!'

Chapter 8

JUST A WOOD

The track up Burnham Mount was strangely inviting in the moonlight, even to Jazzy and Matt, with no sense of smell and almost no hearing compared to Dash. Dash would have found it intoxicating! The long grass on either side rustled with life in a way that it didn't in the daytime. If Dash had come this way, she'd have been detained at every step and still be here. They'd have spotted her, jumping on stuff in the grass, shoving her nose in, snuffing and wagging her tail in that way she did when things were fantastic.

No, she couldn't have been here at all, Matt thought. Jazzy was wrong.

But Jazzy was hurrying up the track, unaware of his doubts.

'Come on!' she shouted over her shoulder. 'I need you to find the way in!'

He wasn't sure if it would still be there. After all, his fairy had gone, and left him with nothing but a stick. Perhaps the scooped-out place in the bushes would have disappeared, too. It was like that old story about the man who finds a singing tortoise. A man finds a singing tortoise in a forest, and tells the king. The king is impressed and commands the man to fetch it. But when he does, the tortoise won't sing: it's just a tortoise. And the king thinks the man has lied, and chops off his head.

If you thought about this in connection with the fairy, there was one good thing. The tortoise was evil and Matt felt his fairy was not. It hadn't played a trick on him; it was he who'd expected too much.

And the place in the thorn bushes was still there.

'You got through *that*?' said Jazzy, and Matt felt a kind of pride that he had. He could see why Jazzy had questioned it, though: it was hard to believe.

'Dash?' he called into the wood, in case she'd come out

and save them the trouble of burrowing in. But nothing happened.

He was glad he had grabbed his coat from the peg in the hall before they'd left. He wrapped it around himself tightly and got down on hands and knees. He pressed his face and chest to the earth – now, in the night, it was cold and damp – and started to squirm his way into the hollow, under the thorns and through. Jazzy, behind, on the track, was silent. He knew not to try to raise his head and look back till he was far enough in, and when he felt it was safe to, he couldn't see her any more.

Would she follow him? he wondered. She'd said that Burnham Wood was haunted. Would she go home? But this had been her idea. Being Jazzy, she'd want to see it through.

Her voice sounded faint and much further off than it could have been really. But he still caught the words: 'Wait for me!'

Then there were sounds of a struggle: small gasps and cries, as the thorns caught her hair.

'Keep your head down!' he called. Hair, clothes and skin. 'Hunch your shoulders!'

Would she regret her idea? It would have been under-standable. But he thought not. And then she was close behind him, saying in a shocked voice, 'Ouch, that *hurt*!' But she didn't go on about it and she didn't mention ghosts.

'What are we waiting for?' she said.

Matt set off on hands and knees, and Jazzy did the same. When he raised himself to a crouching position, so did she. The moon shone down through bare branches above, and everything was touched by its cold, clear light. On the path, even more than on the track, they felt that everything round them rustled and twitched with night-time life. They straightened up.

'It's magic!' breathed Jazzy.

'It's just a wood.'

Matt was wary. She'd laughed at his stick. She'd said did he really mean it had all been for *this*? (And that was even before she'd seen the photo and the caption.)

'It's like *A Midsummer Night's Dream*,' she said now.

'Midsummer?' Matt shivered. 'If only!'

'I mean the play.'

'Oh, here we go! Shakespeare?'

'Yes! There's a wood in it, just outside Athens, with spells and enchantment and fairies!'

She dropped the word in lightly, as if it had no more weight than the others, no strings attached.

Maybe it hadn't. Shakespeare, it seemed, got away with a lot.

Or maybe it had.

And now they had reached the clearing. He wasn't going to tell her, but she knew.

'Is this it? Is this where . . . ? When you came before . . . ?' And then: 'Oh, Matt – *look*!'

They were standing side by side, and he had seen it at once, well before she grabbed his arm.

Something lying at the foot of the great, spreading tree.

Last time he was here, he'd watched Dash on this spot, wagging her tail, in the grip of excitement.

Now she lay still.

Dasher lay stretched out under the tree, in the moonlight, as if she had fallen asleep on a hot summer's day.

'Oh, Matt,' said Jazzy again, and she thought: *They*

didn't take the stick, but they've taken Dash. She thought not of ghosts, but of something less clear, and glanced round in wonder. She trembled. But the wood kept its secrets; there was nothing to see.

'She's asleep,' said Matt, though as he said it, he made a sound like he'd just been punched in the stomach. The sound was a sob.

After a little while, Jazzy said gently, 'Go to her, then.' And when he didn't, she added, 'Or shall I?'

But he went in the end.

He went in silence. He didn't call her name. He didn't even speak to her when he got close. He knelt down beside her.

Jazzy, from where she stood, saw his shoulders fall in like one of those toys which collapse when you press a spring underneath to loosen the cords that hold them up. *He's going to collapse*, she thought, *just like that.*

And then she saw something amazing.

On exactly the spot where Matt had seen the fairy, she too saw something which seemed like magic.

Matt bowed his head towards the dog lying motionless

on the ground, and the dog raised its head! Dash pressed her muzzle to his face! Then she got herself up and was all over him, greeting him, wagging her tail, squirming with pleasure at finding him there.

'She was just asleep,' said Matt again, as they walked down the track again, on their way home.

He'd forgotten to bring Dash's lead, and was carrying her, cradling her in his arms. Every now and then, she heard a noise in the grass and pricked her ears and tried to scramble free, but he held her tight.

He'd said it once too often: just asleep. They both knew there was more to it than that, but neither of them said. Dogs didn't just lie down for a snooze in the middle of a wood, in the night. Jazzy thought again of enchantment and *A Midsummer Night's Dream*.

Neither of them said what both had thought when they'd first seen Dash under the tree.

'Call your mum and dad,' said Jazzy, 'to say we've found her! Call Luke!'

'Luke?' said Matt. 'I'm not calling *him*!'

'Why not? He'd be pleased.'

'Luke doesn't care about anything but his music and his games.'

'He cares about Dash, else why did he go out looking for her, in the village?'

'You call him, then. I'm not going to.'

'I haven't got my phone on me,' Jazzy said, sounding regretful.

Matt, not sounding regretful at all, said, 'Neither have I!'

Chapter 9
PECK, PECK, PECK

Angela Poole was worried.

There was usually something to worry about these days. Since her dad had left, she and her mum spent a lot of time worrying about each other. But today it was something else, and Angela Poole was worried *sick*. She had actually thrown up at breakfast, so now she was in bed, instead of at school. She sat there, propped up with pillows, not reading the books or comics strewn across her duvet, just clutching her iPod and worrying. Worrying about Jazzy. Worrying about Tash.

Jazzy fancied Matt Barker. Everyone said so and the photograph proved it. Perhaps they were actually going out together. Could well be. If they chose to spend their time putting dirt on their faces in somebody's garden, there was no knowing *what* else they might be up to.

Jazzy fancied Matt Barker, the new boy who nobody could work out. And Matt Barker, who was so strange, who spoke of fairies and lied in the Truth Game – Matt Barker, who (Mr McGann had said) loved football, but made no attempt to play – Matt Barker fancied Jazzy. There it was, the fact of it, on the screen in her hand.

It was all very weird. But that wouldn't have mattered, except that if anyone fancied (or was fancied by) anyone else, it had to be Tash. Tash was the bird at the top of the tree, the hen highest up on the perch. She had to peck, to punish, if somebody dared to step out of line.

That was what worried Angela Poole.

'All right up there?' called her mum.

No! she wanted to say. *Not all right – all wrong! It's all getting out of control!* But her mum would have misunderstood and brought her something else to be sick in. And this thing was too big, too bad, to be contained in a washing-up bowl.

Should she talk to a teacher?

Mr McGann not only taught them French, he was their form tutor as well. He often relied on Ange to sort things out. But if she went to him with this, he'd think she was wasting his time. It's *good* that Jazzy likes Matt, he'd probably say. Nobody else does!

Someone had come into school to give them a talk about cyber bullying. You had to report it at once because it could get out of hand so fast. But this wasn't cyber bullying. It was just a photo on Facebook. It was just Tasha Lawes being Tash, and everyone knew what she was like. Jazzy knew best of all. She could perfectly well look after herself.

Angela picked up a comic and rustled the pages to cover the sound of *peck, peck, peck* she could hear in her head.

Chapter 10

THERE ARE MORE THINGS

'I thought you weren't going to come back. After the stick.'

'So did I,' said Jazzy.

'You laughed.'

'I laugh at a lot of things. Haven't you noticed? Mum says you can't laugh too much, but Dad . . . '

'What does he say?' Matt felt sorry for anyone serious, having to live in a family like that.

'He says you can.' She paused. Then she burst out laughing nearly as much as she had when she'd seen the stick. 'But only because he's a dentist! He says it shouldn't be legal to laugh unless you've got perfect teeth!'

When she'd got over that one, 'You don't laugh at any-thing, do you?' she said.

They were sitting on the edge of Matt's bed. His room was already reverting to how it had been before the school trip. Idly, he did some footwork on a crisp packet into which he had recently stuffed other packets and wrap-pers: he coaxed it up off the floor, then suddenly chucked it in the air and sent it sailing into the King Harold bin, which was standing alone in a corner, still practically empty.

He didn't answer her question, but asked another one instead. 'Why *did* you laugh at the stick? It wasn't *funny*.'

'I was angry.' Then she added, 'Not with you. With myself. With the situation. It's good if you can laugh when you're angry. Sometimes you can't.'

Even Matt got what she was talking about: the situation with Tash. She wasn't laughing *that* off – it had gone too far. When he said, 'We could put "LOL" on Facebook,' it wasn't a serious suggestion.

But she replied as if it was.

'No. Remember that talk we got? The woman said you mustn't fan the flames. You've got to be careful not to make things worse.'

So what are you doing now? he wanted to shout. The photo had been a warning. Stop hanging out with weird Matt Barker. He turned to face her. 'Why *have* you come back?'

She laughed at that. 'You mean people might think it's true, that we fancy each other? They've got the wrong end of the stick! I don't fancy *you*!'

Who, then, he wondered? But it wasn't important. 'The stick . . .'

'Wrong end of!' she said.

'No! *My* stick. The one you laughed at. But still you came back . . .'

Jazzy took a deep breath.

'First I came back to help you find Dasher. I heard you call, and I came. Then, when I saw her there in the wood, I knew I'd been wrong to laugh at the stick. There was something funny going on, but not funny LOL.'

Matt could follow all that. He waited.

'*There are more things in heaven and earth than are dreamt of in your philosophy.*'

Now she was talking in riddles again!

'My philosophy?' he said, trying not to sound desperate.

'It's from *Hamlet*,' said Jazzy. 'The play? By—'

'Shakespeare?'

She nodded. 'It means all the things we *know* might not be all there *are*.'

'Oh.'

'It also means –' she looked at him hard – 'there might be something strange in Burnham Wood.'

At this point they heard a noise from next door, a sudden outburst of screaming. '*Scary! Too scary!*' distinctly came through the wall, and a series of terrible roars.

'Nige and Lissy,' said Jazzy, still looking at Matt and dismissing the noise with a wave of her hand. 'Playing lions and sweet little girls.' She was waiting for him to react to her statement.

He dragged his mind back.

Something strange in Burnham Wood. *That* made sense. Something strange. Yes, there was.

'A ghost?' he suggested.

But she threw back at him what he'd said on the coach: 'Ghosts are kids' stuff!'

'What, then?'

'*I* don't know! You tell me!'

('*Teeth and claws!*' from next door.)

He'd seen it and given it a name, the thing in the wood. Which had been his biggest mistake. Anyway, it had died, whatever it was. They were way too late.

The sounds next door subsided and – in the lull – he had an idea.

'What did you mean when you talked about others? How do you know there are more?'

'I don't. I'm just guessing. I'm thinking, how likely is it that there was one single fairy – or whatever – in that whole wood, and you *happened* to see it?'

'It's possible,' he said. He was arguing for the sake of it now – but it was.

'I can't believe it,' said Jazzy. 'And don't forget Dash. *She* knows there's still something, otherwise why did she go back?'

She remembered what she'd imagined before: a swarm of a thousand fairies flowing up the wall of the Barkers' house. 'There must be a thousand sticks in Burnham Wood. No, a million! More! I can't believe yours was different from all the rest. It wouldn't make sense.'

'Nothing does!'

'That's because we don't know enough!' She jumped up. 'We need to research!'

But Matt felt suddenly hopeless. The longer he went without playing football, the less he believed he would ever again. And none of this stuff with Jazzy was helping.

'*Stop! Stop!*' burst out again from next door. '*No tickling!*'

And in the hush that followed, 'Let's forget it,' he said. He looked at the floor.

'I needn't prove anything, really,' he added. 'And you – things can only get worse for you if we go on.'

And quite unexpectedly, Jazzy sat down. She looked at him sadly, wanting to argue but letting the dull, heavy truth sink in. The weight of his words was too much. To go on would be foolish. Dangerous even. *Don't fan the flames.*

She actually opened her mouth to say it: 'You're right, let's give up.'

They came that close.

And that would have been the end of the story. Jazzy and Tash together again. Matt Barker waiting for Mikey, Dip, Joe to come knocking on his door (which they probably would have, sooner or later). Everyone happy ever after. Danger averted, excitement squashed.

What did Burnham Wood matter?

That would have been it, if Matt hadn't opened *his* mouth.

If he'd understood one other thing, if he'd sorted out something four pages back, he'd never have made this big mistake.

'We can't do research, anyway,' he said, 'Luke's playing games on the computer.'

Chapter 11

TILL BIRNAM WOOD

'Go away!' said Luke. 'I'm in the middle of something. It's important.'

On the screen, a woman dressed in armour was leading a dinosaur through a swamp. On Luke's lap, Dash was curled up, asleep. She loved gaming.

'We need to do some research,' said Matt. 'You've already been on there all day.'

'Tough,' said Luke. 'Go away.'

The computer they had to share was tucked away underneath the stairs, off the hall. The space had been a cupboard for coats, but their dad had taken the door off and put in a shelf table, and a chair. The only light was from the screen, which meant that the deepest recesses of the cupboard were in darkness. It made you think of a cave, or the den of a bear.

Luke was the bear – growling, warning them off. When he got like that, there was no point even trying.

'Come on, Jazzy,' said Matt. 'Let's find my mum. She'll sort him out.'

'For God's *sake*!' said Luke, but maybe only because a rock in the swamp had exploded and made the dinosaur rear up, nearly trampling the woman underfoot.

Dash curled up tighter. This was the downside of gaming: people getting angry.

'I'll stay here,' said Jazzy. 'You go.' And when he had, she said to Luke, 'Nige plays that.' She stepped up close and stroked Dasher's head.

Luke looked round.

'I know you have to get to a checkpoint in order to save the game. Otherwise you have to repeat the section. Watch *out*!'

A man with a samurai sword had crept up, but the warrior woman had an axe and they fought and she won. She cut the man down and took his sword and left him, a pile of bleeding limbs, on the ground.

'Good,' said Jazzy.

But Luke only hunched further forward and said, 'Yeah, yeah.'

When Matt and his mum came into the hall, Luke was sitting on the floor, slumped against the wall opposite the computer, with his legs stretched out and his headphones on. Jazzy was on the chair in the den, tapping busily at the keyboard. Dasher was curled up just as before, as if one lap had gone and another had come and she'd never had to move.

'Luke's given us ten minutes,' said Jazzy, 'so we have to be quick!'

'What?' said Matt. 'But how—?'

'Perfect!' said Deborah Barker. 'I was just going to say: in ten minutes, it's tea!'

'Oh, *what*?' said Luke. 'If I'd known, I'd never . . . That's *great*!'

He said it in a voice that would have suited his storming off, but he seemed unable to summon the energy to move.

'You can take yourself off and listen to music in your bedroom, if you like,' said his mum, though without much hope. 'I'll give you a shout when it's time to come down.'

'No *point*!' said Luke. He fiddled about with his iPod.

Deborah turned brightly to Jazzy. 'Would you like to stay for tea?'

Jazzy said yes, thanks, she would – and no, she didn't need to ask at home. They were only having sandwiches that night, so it wouldn't matter. Besides, she and Matt had a lot to get through. Even as she spoke, she was typing.

They googled 'tree spirit', 'wood elf' and 'woodland fairy'.

Jazzy was pleased, because Shakespeare came up (but it wasn't helpful). There was loads of stuff about things called nymphs, which the Ancient Greeks thought lived in woods and were sometimes linked to particular trees. But nothing related to what Matt had seen. They even googled 'Burnham Wood' – and Shakespeare came up *again*!

'Can't get away from him.' Matt was annoyed. 'And look: he can't even spell!'

'*Till Birnam Wood shall come to Dunsinane!*' said Jazzy with reverence. 'It's a different Burnham. Must be somewhere in Scotland. The quote's from *Macbeth*, and that's where *Macbeth* is set.'

'Well, it's no use to us, then,' Matt said crossly.

'It's what the witches say to Macbeth when they're predicting his future: he's not going to die till Birnam Wood takes itself to Dunsinane . . .'

'Well, he's going to live for ever, then: woods can't move!'

'That's exactly what *he* thinks!' said Jazzy, in triumph. 'But he's wrong!'

'We're all going to die,' said Luke unexpectedly, from the floor. 'Specially Matt, if he doesn't let me get back on there before tea.'

Matt ignored him. That wood in Scotland (or theirs, back here) was more likely to move than his brother.

Jazzy had clicked on images, and they found themselves looking at photos of bearded old men – and topless women with long flowing hair – carved into tree trunks. It was embarrassing.

'Try, "wood fairy stick",' said Matt quickly. Jazzy did, but all that came up were sites selling decorative items made of bark and one that told you how to build a fairy house in the trees.

'Go back to wood nymphs,' said Matt. 'We ought to go through them, one by one, to make sure.'

There were loads. And they all had long, difficult names. But Jazzy pounced on details here and there that seemed to fit.

'Look!' she said. ' "Normally considered to be very shy creatures" . . . and here: "if a tree died, its nymph died as well . . . the Greek gods punished anyone who harmed trees without first propitiating the tree-nymphs."'

Neither of them knew what 'propitiating' meant, but they could guess.

'We *haven't* "harmed trees", though,' Matt objected.

'You stole the twig! Maybe you'll be punished!' She gathered up Dash in her arms and shrank away from him, making out he might be struck by lightning.

Matt was speechless. Then, 'Rubbish!' he exclaimed. 'Taking the twig did no harm – and the tree isn't dying – and Greek gods don't exist!'

He grabbed Dash and held her himself, as if daring non-existent gods to strike him. They didn't.

'There! See! All rubbish, like I said. You can't seriously think I saw a tree nymph!'

'I don't,' said Jazzy. 'It was just an example.'

'What were you two doing on the computer?' said Malcom Barker at tea.

'Research,' said Jazzy, and then straight away, 'into fairies.'

Matt was surprised she'd said. In the moment that followed, the only sound came from Luke, who was eating with his mouth open.

Jazzy laughed, briefly. 'My sister eats like that. She sounds *just* like that!'

Luke shut his mouth, but looked as if he might open it again to speak.

'Why were you looking up fairies, Jazzy?' said Deborah Barker hastily.

'I'm acting the part of one, in a Shakespeare play.' The statement was not untrue.

'Yeah, yeah, *A Midsummer Night's Dream*,' said Luke rudely, and forgot to close his mouth again. Matt was surprised for a second time: not by the mouth, but the knowledge of Shakespeare.

'No!' said Jazzy. '*The Tempest*!'

'There aren't any fairies in that,' said Luke.

'There's Ariel. He's a spirit. Same difference. Anyway, the whole setting is magic. *The isle is full of noises*.' She burst out laughing and looked directly at Luke. 'Like this room!'

He shut his mouth and glowered at her, considering counter-attack. Then, luckily, the doorbell rang. Dash rushed out to wait on the mat.

'Luke, will you get that?' said Deborah.

'Why me?'

'Because you've finished.'

He pushed his chair back clumsily (Jazzy couldn't tell whether this was deliberate) and stomped after Dash. They heard the front door open and a high, piping voice said something ending in 'lovely dog!' Luke came back with Melissa O'Hanlon attached to one of his fingers. He (though not she) looked awkward. With her other hand, she was gripping Dash's collar.

'Jazzy, we've got sambidges!' said Melissa.

'I know, don't make any for me: I'm eating here.'

'But Jazzy, we've got them for *you*!'

'Oh dear,' said Deborah.

'Don't worry,' said Jazzy, 'I'll take them to school tomorrow and have them for lunch. Lissy, go back and tell Mum to put them in cling film.'

While Melissa took in this instruction, Luke tried to pull his finger free.

'Why are you doing that?' She looked up into his face. 'Don't you like holding hands?'

'You don't need to hold on to Dash,' he muttered.

'I'm ready to go now,' said Melissa. 'Come on,' and she led them both away.

'Oh dear,' said Deborah again. 'I should have—'

'Really, it's fine,' said Jazzy. 'Don't think any more about it. As I was saying, in *The Tempest* I'm a fairy –'

Luke came back in – 'or a spirit – whatever – that's been shut up for years in one of the trees on the island. There's all different kinds of spirits, you know!'

'Fascinating!' said Deborah.

'Yeah, yeah,' said Luke, collapsing into his chair.

'So what kind is yours?' said Malcolm. 'Did you come to any conclusions?'

'Jazzy thought it might be a wood nymph,' said Matt.

'I didn't,' said Jazzy. 'That was just an example. To be honest, we got confused.'

Malcolm suddenly sat up straight in his chair and tapped the side of his cup with a teaspoon, like someone with something important to say.

Jazzy waited expectantly.

Matt knew him better.

Malcolm coughed.

'I've got it!' He held up the teaspoon. 'It's obvious!' He waved the spoon about, to conduct his own words: '*You're barking up the wrong tree!*'

Chapter 12

TAMING THEM

The pale grey twigs of the ash tree bear black conical buds. They are set in opposite pairs and the tip of each twig ends in a single flattened bud, which is much larger than the rest. The ash tree does not open its leaves until late April.

BBC Science and Nature Homepage

'That's it!' shouted Jazzy, when she read the page. 'I'm *glad* it's an ash.'

It was like when she'd said she was glad he'd said 'fairy'.

'I guessed it was going to be oak, but an ash is less obvious.' That was Jazzy all over.

'I don't see what difference it makes,' said Matt. He

had picked the stick out of the King Harold bin, where, as he had known it would, it had rested safely since the day he had put it there: the day he had banned his mum from touching anything in his room ever again. Now he'd brought it down to the computer.

Malcolm Barker had said they should start by researching trees – which existed – rather than fairies, which (he said) didn't.

'There are the black buds!' said Jazzy, still excited.

They both looked down at the stick in Matt's hand: real enough, though (as they well knew by now) *just* a stick.

'How does it help, knowing what kind of tree it's from?' said Matt.

'It doesn't – directly – but it's background knowledge. It starts to build up a picture. And it's – respectful. We should find out the name of every tree in the wood!'

It sounded hopeless.

To get back on track, Matt changed the search terms. 'Let's check out more nymphs!'

But it didn't head her off: 'We need to do more research, yes –'

Matt was googling a site about butterflies (there was one called a wood nymph) –

'– but not here. Not like that.'

He went to another, on hummingbirds, since, it seemed, a wood nymph was one of those, too.

'*There are more things in heaven and earth than are on the internet!*'

Matt stopped and stared. 'Is that in *Hamlet?*'

'Pretty much. Come on, we need to go back to Burnham Wood!'

'But why? Just because it's an ash tree . . .'

'We need to identify *all* the trees. Bring your phone!'

'But you said—!'

'Bring the stick, then! Come *on!*'

Poppy O'Hanlon said if they were going for a walk, they should take Melissa. And Matt took Dash. That's how there came to be four of them on the track up Burnham Mount.

Dasher was still on the lead because that was what Melissa wanted – she loved having Dash – and Dash herself didn't seem to mind. She probably hardly noticed, thought Matt, since Melissa went everywhere she went, stopped when she stopped, never tugged, never pulled. Every time Dash stuck her nose in some grass, Melissa made a show of putting her hands on her hips, like a disapproving parent. 'Matt! She's sniffing again!' she called, in delight. But when they got to the way in under the bushes, he unclipped the lead and let Dash go first. She disappeared immediately and they heard a pheasant squawk.

'That's what you have to do,' he told Melissa. 'Not chase pheasants, I mean. Squeeze through there. That's where we're going.'

'Not to the Stone?' said Melissa. 'Not to play *I'm the King of the Castle*?' But when they got down in the earth, she was thrilled. By the time they reached the clearing, she had blood on her cheek and her T-shirt was torn, but she wasn't crying.

'Lovely place!' she breathed. She began gathering branches to make a den.

*

Hundreds of soot-black buds were breaking open all over their tree. Their *ash* tree. Sprays of new leaves were appearing and everything seemed very satisfactory. But the tree beside it was a different kind. Its leaves were already out in full and its bark was ridged both vertically and across. It wasn't even half the size of the ash – but then nor was anything else round the clearing.

'Get your phone out!' said Jazzy. 'Let's see what it is!'

Matt had his phone in his right-hand pocket, the stick in his left. He got out the phone.

'That's odd,' he said. 'No signal. Try yours.'

She did and it was the same.

They both looked about them in silence and felt for a moment how strange the place was. Although it was lit by bright spring sunshine, although Melissa was humming a tune, they felt cut off from normal things.

They both shivered.

But Jazzy said briskly, 'All right, put your phone away. Get out the stick.' Malcolm Barker had said to begin by researching trees, but if they couldn't . . . The stick might be better. It certainly seemed more in tune with the clearing than their phones had been.

Her tone broke the spell. Matt held the stick in his hand and felt silly.

'Like you said, it's just a stick, and this –' he waved vaguely around and asserted (despite what he'd felt a minute before) – 'is just a wood.'

Which seemed to make Jazzy lose all patience. 'How can you *say* that?' She was glaring right at him. She actually stamped her foot in frustration. 'How do you know? How can you say what's here and what's not?'

He opened his mouth but she went on.

'How many birds d'you think there are here? Five hundred? Five thousand? How many insects? But would you go home saying no, you'd heard a few pheasants, seen an earwig or two, that was all? Would you say, just because you'd not *seen* them, the others weren't there?'

Matt had been watching Melissa beginning to make a wigwam structure, but now he looked at Jazzy. 'You're not talking about nymphs?'

'No! When I said . . . that was just an example . . . Oh, never mind.'

He waited.

'All those birds, all those insects,' she said, calming down, 'they're examples, too. They're shy.'

He didn't point out that nymphs were shy themselves, according to Wikipedia.

Jazzy finished, 'They're shy – but they're there.'

Far off, in another part of the wood, Dash barked.

'Call her, Matt!' said Melissa, but he didn't. He pictured her in some secret place, madly wagging her tail at – what? But the only way to find out would be to go and see, and the only path leading out of the clearing was the one they'd come in by. And anyway, Jazzy didn't seem to be listening.

'Earwigs are shy?' he continued.

'*They* wouldn't call it shy,' she said.

'They wouldn't call it anything!'

'They wouldn't call it shy – they just don't show themselves.' She looked at him almost fiercely. 'But *they're there*.'

And now 'they' were not earwigs.

Jazzy proposed that they set up a regular watch. She'd worked it all out. If you want to tame something wild, she said, you first have to get it to trust you. And the way to do that is be there again and again, always the same.

She pushed Matt towards the trunk of the tree. 'We'll sit here –' she pulled him down on to a root ('Get off!') – 'for an hour after school every day and the same hour on Saturday and Sunday. Slowly they'll see we mean no harm.'

Now they were both sitting, side by side, at the foot of the tree. It was very uncomfortable, Matt felt, and not just because the roots were hard. But Jazzy seemed too taken up with her plan to notice. 'That's why a robin will come and perch on a gardener's spade. It thinks the gardener's part of the garden. It actually does.'

'No, it doesn't,' said Matt. 'It thinks he might dig up a worm.'

'"He *or she*",' began Jazzy. 'My mum says –' Then she stopped herself. 'Yes! You're right! If you offer a gift – that's even better. Food is good.'

But neither of them could think what might possibly count as food in this case. Matt couldn't imagine his fairy having eaten anything at all. 'They probably eat whatever the trees eat: stuff in the earth, that the roots suck up.'

'We could bring them compost!' said Jazzy. She laughed.

The only thing (and it wasn't food) they could think to offer was the stick. True, the fairies hadn't come to claim it, but that didn't mean . . . Again Jazzy remembered her vision of a load of them swarming up the wall. She couldn't get that out of her head: the dark shadow flowing up towards Matt's window.

'They might be pleased to see it again,' said Matt. 'You never know.'

So he dropped the stick on the ground, somewhere (he hoped) near the spot where he'd first seen it fall.

They called Melissa over, to point it out and say not to touch it. She was very understanding.

'Is it magic?' she asked.

'No. Well, maybe. Is your den magic?' asked Matt, to be nice.

'My den?' She laughed, just like Jazzy. 'It's my *den*!'

Which he didn't understand.

It certainly didn't look magic. Of course she hadn't been doing it long, but it didn't even look much like a den. It looked like a pile of sticks that someone had thrown together for a bonfire. But Melissa seemed happy enough. She went back to it now and examined it closely, then adjusted a twig.

'The *wood's* magic!' she called to them, over her shoulder. Matt shrugged. But Jazzy looked up sharply, then frowned and squinted into the trees.

'You should get her to be more quiet,' said Matt, a while later. 'Nothing shy is going to come out with her crashing around like that.'

'She isn't!' said Jazzy defensively. 'But even if she was . . . They have to get used to us *as we are*. If we're going to come back again and again, we have to act the same every time. Anyway, we know they don't mind noise: you said Dash was *barking* at the one you saw.'

Strangely, as she said this, Dash barked again, still a long way off.

This time they both fell silent and found themselves looking towards the sound. But Dash was unreachable. Both of them knew.

'D'you mean we're going to bring Melissa every time we come here?' said Matt, to distract their attention.

They could come here for weeks and see nothing. They could come forever. What Matt saw now was a football, suspended before him, in the air; it was getting smaller as he watched.

'What about Tasha?' he said. 'If we come here so often, she's bound to notice.'

'Tash fancies Nige,' said Jazzy all of a sudden. 'She wants to go out with him.'

'Great,' said Matt, 'that'll keep her busy.'

'No, no, it won't, because Nige isn't interested. That makes Tash worse. She's jealous. That's why she posted that stupid photo . . .'

'But that was of you and me! Not *Nige*!'

'I know. But it still makes her mad, us getting along.'

Matt didn't know what to say. He hadn't bargained

for any of this, yet here he was entangled in girls' stuff. It was unfair.

'The photo,' said Jazzy, 'has made her *much* worse.'

'She took it herself!' he exclaimed. 'She must know it means nothing!'

'But the caption . . . '

'*She wrote it!* She can't believe her own stupid lie!'

'Still,' Jazzy said quietly. 'We have to be careful.'

'We could just give up.'

This seemed to bring her back to herself.

'No!' she said, with all her old spirit. 'Not now! I want to see one!' She jumped to her feet. 'I want to see at least what you saw. The plan will work.' She bit her lip. 'It can't take long. And then we can get back to normal. Only nothing will ever be normal again. All my life, I'll know Shakespeare was right! *There are more things . . .*'

Tasha Lawes was a patient person. More patient than Jazzy, in certain ways. She could bide her time. But only up to a point. She could wait, but didn't like to feel her generous spirit was being abused. Right now she was waiting to see if Jazzy was going to toe the line. She hoped she was – and not just because that would save her (Tash Lawes) trouble.

Jazzy should behave for her own sake.

It would save her getting hurt.

Chapter 13

OBSERVERS

The next day, as she sat in position beside Matt, Jazzy found an unusual leaf.

Melissa was working on her den, not humming but actually talking now – to herself or, more likely, to some imaginary friend. They didn't bother to listen. Neither did they bother to mention Matt's stick, which was just where he'd left it.

It wasn't a good sign.

Jazzy's leaf was only unusual because it was bright green and small and young – and shouldn't have fallen at this time of year. It was spring, not autumn.

'Too young to die!' she joked, twiddling its stalk between finger and thumb.

It had come from the smaller tree next to the ash, that she'd hoped to identify yesterday. 'I bet *that's* an oak,' she said now. 'In fact, I *know* it's an oak! I'm certain.'

'*How* d'you know?' said Matt.

Jazzy held the leaf so close up to her face that she almost went cross-eyed.

'It's telling me!' she said. 'It's sending a message!'

Matt was startled.

Jazzy began dancing the leaf in the air, and talking to it in much the same tones as Melissa was using as she pottered about.

'Really?' she said. 'You grew from an acorn? How long did it take? Look – here's Matt. Tell him—'

She danced the leaf in front of his face but he batted her hand away.

'Stupid!' he said. 'If you're not going to take this seriously . . .'

'Seriously – it's an oak leaf,' said Jazzy. 'It looks exactly the same as the ones on the National Trust sticker in our car!'

Matt snatched it out of her fingers. 'I'll take it home and show Dad. He'll know.'

Malcolm Barker owned a second-hand bookshop. He was gloomy on the subject. 'No one wants books any more, new or second-hand,' he'd say. But it meant he knew a lot of odd things, which could be useful. He knew straight away that the little green leaf Matt showed him had come from an oak tree.

'I brought it home,' said Matt, 'because my phone wouldn't work in the wood.'

'Phone wouldn't work, eh?' said Dad. 'I know what you need!' He practically skipped down the passage. 'Follow me!'

But Mum intercepted them in the hall.

'Matt, I meant to tell you, while you were out, some people called round. Three boys. I asked their names, and I think they said Joe and Michael and – Dick, would it be?'

Matt was glad Jazzy wasn't there. She'd have laughed at that.

'What did they want?' he said, sitting down suddenly on the stairs.

Dad had gone into the living room, full of impatience to show him whatever it was. They could hear him exclaiming over something, pleased and excited.

'What did they want?' Mum repeated. 'Well, obviously, you! They said they'd come round again, sometime. Oh, yes, and one of them had a ball . . .'

'Matt, where are you?' called Dad. 'Come in here!'

And when Matt did, he found Dad reaching up to the top shelf in the alcove, where a row of neat little books with short, fat spines and white covers were lined up next to each other. They clearly all belonged to a series, and Matt, who had good eyesight, could see from where he stood by the sofa that each had printed on its spine, 'Observer's' something. *Observer's Dogs*, *Observer's Astronomy*, *Observer's Common Fungi*.

'*Observer's Trees*!' said Dad, and brought it down, sounding really smug. Matt couldn't see why. It was old and tatty, but Dad was behaving as if it was gold. 'They don't publish these any more, but you'll never find better. Here, take it. It'll fit in a pocket.'

It sat in Matt's hand, a compact little hardback. Though

the title lettering was faded, it had a proper paper jacket. It belonged in a museum, thought Matt, never mind his dad's shop. But he couldn't share Dad's excitement.

Mum stuck her head around the door.

'They'll come back?' he said dully.

'I doubt it,' said Dad. 'But look on the bright side. We've got this one – and those –' he waved up to the shelf – 'and if more come my way, I'll snap them up!'

'Oh, *Malcolm*!' said Mum. 'He's not talking about *books*!'

'Look what Dad gave me,' he said next day, as they sat side by side on the roots of the ash tree and Melissa worked on her den.

'Oh, *cute*!' said Jazzy when she saw the book.

Underneath the picture (of a tree) on the front, it said, 'Fully illustrated in colour and black & white: 106 SPECIES DESCRIBED'.

'I know!' Jazzy said. 'Let's look for them! Let's find them all!'

But Matt was dismissive. 'There aren't one hundred and six *trees* round this clearing, let alone one hundred and six species! There's this one and that one.' He glanced at the oak. 'That's two!'

'More than *that*!' said Jazzy. She swept her hand round, pointing out trees at random. 'There! Ten!'

'But they won't all be different.'

'They might be,' said Jazzy. 'And if they're not, we'll just have to go further in.'

'We can't – no paths.'

She chose to ignore him. 'I bet we can find ten kinds, if we try!'

But the trees she'd spotted at first weren't all different; Matt was right. They were oak, ash and something the book said was sycamore (five of those). And when they tried to go further in, he was right again: they couldn't. There really were no paths out of the clearing, except their own. Everywhere else was just briars and thorns.

'Oh, be *quiet*, Melissa!' snapped Jazzy, to express her exasperation. 'You're getting on my nerves! Tell your friends the party's over: it's time to go home!'

'But it wasn't a party and they *are* at home!' said Melissa, sounding offended.

'Just shut up, I mean.'

'*You* shut up!'

'Right!' said Jazzy. 'You can help us. Now! We bring you here to be nice, not to have you going on all the time. Come away from there and help us look for an opening in these bushes.'

Melissa complained.

'I want to go on with my den,' she said. 'Anyway, there isn't an opening.'

'There must be. Dash comes and goes all the time.'

'Dash doesn't need *openings*. She goes where she likes.'

This was probably true. Jazzy and Matt knew Dash was at home in the place, like *they* never would be. They felt themselves foreigners here, beside her.

'Well, you can help look for trees, then,' said Jazzy.

'Look for *trees*?' said Melissa. (And it did sound daft.)

'After, we'll take you to play on the Stone,' said Matt quickly.

'Different kinds, I mean,' Jazzy went on. 'There must be some, growing a bit further in – but not too far in to see from here.'

And this time she was right.

Matt gave Melissa the book to hold and she matched the trees they spotted with the trees in the pictures. She liked the colour plates best, which were drawings, not photos.

They worked their way round the edge of the clearing, peering into the bushes, and found quite a few more trees that way. None was as big as their ash and many were only young, like the oak, but there were a nice lot of different kinds. Jazzy grew more cheerful.

'Remember, we only need ten!'

'Why ten?' said Matt. 'What's so special about ten? Just because you said . . .'

'Ten would mean *species diversity*,' said Jazzy. It wouldn't exactly, but it would in a way. She'd heard of species diversity from Nige, who'd done it in science. Nige had asked her to test him only last week, with a big floppy book called *Biology: Understanding Our World*. She'd sat with the book in her lap and looked down at page 12 and said, 'Tell me what species diversity is.'

'Species diversity is a healthy range of different species,'

Nige had chanted, 'enabling a natural environment to thrive.'

'Tell me what "thrive" is.'

'Grow, develop,' Nige had said. 'Have a viable future.'

'Tell me what "viable" is'

But Nige had snatched the book from her hands and playfully walloped her with it, ending the session.

Neither Nige nor the book had actually said what a 'healthy range' of species was. But ten sounded right. And by that reckoning, Burnham Wood had a sporting chance. It would *probably* thrive: they found nine different species of tree for definite – plus one that was iffy.

The nine were oak, ash and sycamore, elder and alder, hawthorn and holly, hazel and sloe.

The tenth was a spindle tree.

Maybe.

Jazzy said it was, Matt said it wasn't. The book said spindles were rare, which Matt pointed out in support of his claim: 'It's an alder gone wrong!'

'We'll know for sure in the autumn,' said Jazzy. 'The book says if it's a spindle tree, it'll have "pale crimson" seed cases then.'

How strange that sounded. Could you *have* pale crimson?

Will we still be coming in autumn? thought Matt.

But the spindle, the tenth kind of tree, was important to Jazzy.

'*Pale crimson*,' she said in her most insistent voice. 'Don't forget!'

Cycling away from Burnham Mount, Tasha Lawes had a fixed expression. Her soft hair flowed out behind her, and she looked grim. Her arms were scratched and her shoes were dirty, but that was only part of the reason.

She was cycling to Kezzia's house, in too much of a hurry to clean herself up.

Chapter 14

FUNNY DOLLS

It was the fifth day of going and sitting in the wood when Matt's doorbell rang. He was just putting Dash's lead on. (*What is it with this house?* he thought. *People always seem to come in and go out at just the same time!*)

He opened the door, and it was Mikey, Dip, Joe. Mikey was holding a football. Dip squatted down at once to stroke Dash.

'Want to come for a kickabout?' said Joe.

Matt felt he'd never wanted anything more in his life. It was like being offered your favourite sweet: just thinking about it, you *taste* it and spit flows into your mouth.

'No, thanks,' he said. 'Got to walk the dog.'

'You said *what*?' Jazzy cried incredulously and her eyes were big, even for her. 'You're weird, Matt Barker, like everyone says.'

'Oh, for—' He couldn't explain.

'I can't believe you messed up *again*!'

'I had to come here, didn't I?'

'You could have called me! You could have texted! I'd have understood, you know I would. What I can't understand is why you sent them away!'

Matt reached forward from where they sat, and picked up his stick, which, ever since he had carefully left it for the fairies, had remained untouched. He flung it angrily into the undergrowth. Jazzy didn't stop him.

'You're like Hamlet!' she said.

'Oh, for— *Shakespeare!*' he burst out. 'I've *had it* with him!'

They fell silent. Melissa came round the side of her den (which had grown, but still looked like a bonfire) and stared at them anxiously, sucking her thumb.

'Anyway,' Matt said, more quietly, 'how can a person

be like a play?'

'Hamlet's not just the name of the play, it's the name of a character as well. He gives it its name. It's him you're like.'

'Was he weird?' said Matt, bitterly.

'Yes,' said Jazzy. 'He really wanted to do something and he kept just putting it off.'

'What was it?'

'Killing his uncle.'

Matt burst out laughing. 'I haven't even got any uncles! And anyway – well, it's not the same thing *at all*!'

Melissa went back to work on her den.

'It is, in a way, though,' said Jazzy. 'The thing about putting something off. He spends the whole play not doing what he knows he must.'

They were silent again, for a time, then Matt said, 'Perhaps he's afraid. If it's really important, perhaps he's afraid it might go wrong.'

Jazzy looked at him shrewdly. 'What are you saying?'

'Just – I can see where he's coming from. It's a risk. If it doesn't work out for him, he'll have blown it. That's all.'

'How about this?' Jazzy said suddenly. 'How if we keep watch in shifts? You know, take turns to come here. Then you'd have time to play football.' She paused. 'They're all right – Mikey, Dip, Joe.' She gave him a quick little smile. 'You'll be fine.'

'But you said it had to be the same each day. You know, both of us here, blending in.'

Jazzy shrugged. 'It'll still be OK. And I'd like time off, too. Tash . . .' She stopped and looked worried. 'I need to hang out with them more.' She sounded like someone who'd just been told by the doctor she needed to take more medicine. 'It would be better for me if I didn't come here *every* day.'

That was the day they heard something, somewhere off among the trees, that made them fall silent and look at each other in dismay.

'What was that?' said Matt.

But both of them knew.

Someone, somewhere, had – quite unmistakably – laughed.

Having neither seen nor heard anything out of the ordinary since they'd been coming, they'd both have loved to believe it was fairy laughter – but they knew it wasn't. Though quickly suppressed, the laugh had been human. And girlish.

'Melissa!' said Jazzy, with a little too much relief.

'Yes, Melissa!'

'She must have gone back down the path without telling us!'

'Yes!' said Matt.

'That's what! For goodness sake! MELISSA!'

She called down the path but – '*Boo!*' – Melissa star-jumped out from behind her den.

Jazzy was unaccountably angry. 'Shh!' Her voice sounded harsh and unkind. 'Don't shout!'

'*You* did, Jazzy! More louder than me!'

'Not "more louder"—'

'You *did*!'

Jazzy drew in her breath. 'Well, that was because I thought you were over there.' She pointed. 'Just now, you were.' She paused. 'Weren't you? How did you do that?'

'Magic!' Melissa laughed gleefully. It was what Nige said when he made her spoon disappear at the table. She was playing a game.

But Jazzy was still cross.

'We're not coming here tomorrow.' She broke the news roughly, making it sound like a punishment, something she'd just thought up. 'Matt's still coming, but we're not. We'll come the day after that, on our own, and Matt after that – and then us – and then Matt. From now on, we won't ever come together.' She knew it was mean.

'Not Dash?' said Melissa.

'No,' said Jazzy. 'Not Dash. We're not going to come with Dash ever again.'

Melissa's face crumpled and she started to cry.

When Dash herself turned up and looked at them each in turn with her soft, anxious eyes, it only made things worse. Melissa put her arms round the dog and sobbed.

In the end, they had to promise to come all together one more time, and only then did she cheer up.

*

Melissa was running ahead, towards the clearing, her short legs working hard to jump her over fallen branches. Dash was with her, keeping pace.

The clearing was still too far off to see, and Melissa disappeared, but they heard her give a cry of surprise – and then she was running back towards them. When she reached them again, she was out of breath and excited. Dash was panting.

'Oh, Jazzy,' she said, 'funny dollies! There's *dollies*!'

'What d'you mean, dollies? Where?' Jazzy asked sharply.

'Come and see!' She ran back the way she'd come and Matt and Jazzy quickened their pace. They'd waited so long for something to happen, but both felt this wasn't it. Melissa didn't know much, but she could tell a doll from a fairy.

They stopped when they reached the clearing, just where Matt had stopped that first day, and looked across to the foot of the ash tree. Sunlight was slanting down, now as then, but it fell on something new, something wrong.

Not one thing, in fact, but two, clamped together,

though they might as well have been one: both were pink.

'Don't touch!' barked Jazzy – she didn't know why – as Melissa went forward. She was in detective-inspector mode: this wasn't their lovely clearing now, but a crime scene. Melissa didn't argue. She waited in silence and they all proceeded in a tight little group.

The pink things were plastic: two pink baby dolls, chubby arms and legs outstretched. One lay on top of the other; the one underneath was on its back. Their heads were both turned to one side, to face outwards, but their faces were covered by roughly cut circles of paper, stuck down in some way. Apart from the circles of paper, they had nothing on.

The circles of paper were replacement faces – photos of faces. Photos that Jazzy and Matt had seen before.

'Dirty,' said Melissa. 'Dirty faces.' She bent down and picked up the doll on top and Jazzy didn't try to stop her now. 'Matt! It's you!' She picked up the other one. 'Jazzy!' And then, 'Are they magic?'

'No,' said Jazzy and Matt together. 'They're not.'

Chapter 15

BABES IN THE WOOD

Angela was back at school, but she was still worried. Worried, if anything, *more* than when she'd been off sick. Jazzy O'Hanlon had been weird since France and she seemed to be getting weirder. If she fancied Matt Barker, why couldn't she *say*? Why didn't she see him in break times? Why didn't she sit with him at lunch? That was what Katy Arbuthnot and Jack Beeson did, and they all understood.

But Jazzy didn't even speak to Matt Barker at school.

People said they kissed in the woods, but at school they had nothing to do with each other. Matt Barker spent break times and lunchtimes alone. Jazzy spent them with Tash and the rest, chatting and having a laugh, as if nothing had changed.

And Angela knew that *that* was the problem.

Tash wanted Jazzy O'Hanlon to admit what was going on – and, what's more, she would make her, whatever it took. That's what was frightening Angela Poole.

Everyone had to submit to Tash in the end.

So Angela made a decision. She would tell. Or, at least, she would talk. Not to her mum or to Mr McGann – not to any grown-up. To Tash? No!

Angela Poole would talk to Jazzy.

She would use words she'd learnt from Amanda, the counsellor person who talked to her and her mum every Tuesday night. She would try to talk some sense into her, because Ange liked Jazzy and wanted to help – and she knew that the only person who could save the situation was Jazzy herself.

And when it got worse, the situation, as it did very soon (even as Ange was having these thoughts, Tash was reaching for her phone), her resolve only strengthened.

But she couldn't talk to Jazzy at once because Jazzy and everyone else had gone home.

That's where they were when they went on Facebook and saw the new photo uploaded by Tash.

It didn't surprise Jazzy and Matt, but still they were shocked.

It shocked Angela *deeply*.

To get dirty in someone's garden was one thing. To get dirty out in the countryside – with no clothes on – was another. And the fact they were pictured as pink baby dolls made it worse.

It made it grotesque.

'Babes in the Wood,' said the caption.

Ange had to talk to Jazzy ASAP.

'Mum,' said Jazzy, 'has anything bad ever happened to you? Really bad?'

'Yes!' said Poppy O'Hanlon. 'My alizarin crimson's gone missing!'

Poppy was going through a phase of painting big, bright, splodgy flowers – to match her name, as people said. She painted them in her tiny studio, overlooking the garden, on the ground floor.

They were in there now. Jazzy was sitting on her mum's painting stool, which was tall and a bit unstable, and Poppy was spinning round, grabbing things, looking under piles of paper. The studio was an awful mess and she was making it worse.

She picked up a long, flat, rectangular box and shoved it at Jazzy.

'Look at that!'

Inside, there were tubes of paint in little compartments. Unlike the rest of the studio, they appeared to be neatly arranged. They'd been put in order of colour: all the blues, all the greens, all the reds together. But in between scarlet and American rose, there was a gap.

'Someone's been in here!' said Poppy. 'Alizarin Crimson's been taken!' She made it sound as if someone had kidnapped an exotically named child. Although she'd opted for art and not acting, she could still do drama.

'Lissy and Nige are painting something,' said Jazzy.

'But it's a secret. They're in Lissy's room, but you mustn't go in.'

It was Poppy's birthday next week. Jazzy herself hadn't yet made a card.

'Right!' said Poppy immediately. '*Nigel!*' She rushed out and carried on calling in her most threatening voice, as she climbed the stairs.

Jazzy wasn't worried. Lissy and Nige could look after themselves. This sort of rumpus was always blowing up. Lissy's room was directly above the studio, and already Jazzy could hear something heavy being dragged across the floor. By the time Poppy reached the landing, she was too late and could only shout, 'Let me in!' and thump her fists on the barricaded door. She could be some time.

Jazzy let her mind wander. She'd come to ask her mum's advice but didn't know how to. Everyone thought she was so independent, so confident, so bold. No one would guess that right now she was *frightened*. Would her mum guess? Did she want her to, even?

It wasn't Tash she was frightened of, exactly.

It was the unknown.

(Overhead, her mum growled, 'I'll huff and I'll puff . . .' and Lissy screamed with delight.)

But *what* unknown? Not whatever it was in Burnham Wood: that was exciting! When she was there, in the clearing, listening to Dash bark at *something*, not knowing what it was, it was scary but thrilling as well. But now she was here at home, with the picture on Facebook going round in her head, the fear of not being Tash's best friend (having been it for such a long time) seemed more real. Forget Burnham Wood. Forget asking her mum what to do. She'd decided already.

Relieved, she looked round the studio and caught sight of the paints in the long, flat box. She was still looking at them when Poppy came back.

'They say they need it and I'll get it back soon,' her mum complained. 'But I need it now!'

'Have you got *pale* crimson?' said Jazzy. 'I can't see it here.'

'No, I have not! And if I had, it would be no good. I need . . .'

'Yes, yes, I know. I was only wondering what pale would be like.'

Poppy O'Hanlon eyed Jazzy, perched so precariously on her stool, and suddenly thought how unsafe she looked.

'You all right, my love? Is anything wrong?'

'I'm fine. It's just that I'd like to know—'

'Pale crimson, you say? Well, I'm not sure that even makes sense, because crimson is *dark*. It's like saying light black: you can't have *light black*. And I don't think pale crimson exists.'

'Oh, it does!' Jazzy said – with such force that she wobbled alarmingly on her stool.

'Be careful!' said Poppy.

But Jazzy repeated, 'It definitely does!'

Poppy was taken aback and tactfully turned to examine her easel. Neither said anything more for a while. Then Poppy coughed. 'Anyway, what were you asking? Before all this?'

'Can't remember,' said Jazzy. 'It wasn't important.'

'It sounded important.'

'Well, it wasn't.'

Poppy looked at her sternly.

So, 'At least,' Jazzy added, 'it *was*, but it's not any more.'

Poppy kept on looking.

Jazzy sighed, for effect. 'All I said was, has anything bad ever happened to you? But it's OK, I don't need to know.'

Poppy burst out laughing.

'You can't get to my age – forty-seven next week! – and answer no to that question! Where shall I start? My grandparents died. My cat got run over. I broke my leg. I deliberately (yes, *deliberately*) dropped your Uncle Tim's brand-new watch out of a boat in the Mediterranean!'

'But wasn't that worse for *him*?' Jazzy put in.

'No, not in the long run, I can tell you! It was far worse for me.'

She paused, remembering Tim's watch and how it had instantly sunk from sight – and Jazzy imagined the shoals of bright fishes, the dolphins, the sharks, all waiting below.

'But at school?' she said before she could stop herself. 'Anything bad happen there?'

'I failed my exams,' Poppy said promptly. 'Is that bad enough?'

She searched Jazzy's face and spoke slowly and carefully now. 'My best friend turned against me.' She was looking right into her daughter's eyes. '*That* was bad.'

'What did you do?'

'What did I do to make her, or what did I try to do when she did?'

'What did you do to make things go back to how they were before?'

'Well, I *should* have asked myself whether I even wanted them to go back. That would have saved a lot of heartache.'

'But you didn't?'

'No, I panicked.'

'And?'

'Did the wrong thing.'

'And after that?'

'Did the wrong thing again! Can you believe it? Only *then* did I see that she *wasn't* my friend. Never had been. Then I got angry.'

'Was that the end?'

'Well, I had to get *really* angry – you and I do anger well – before I got over it and was able to move on. All in all, it was a long, hard road. I only hope—'

But she never said what she only hoped because just then there was a sharp *CRACK!* and something heavy and hard hit the window. The glass didn't actually break, but the sound was so shocking that both of them jumped and Jazzy fell right off her stool, to the floor.

When they looked, there was something dangling down outside, on a long piece of string. The top of the string was out of sight, but they saw what was tied to the bottom – what it was that had crashed against the glass: a tube of paint.

The tube of alizarin crimson hadn't broken the window, but Poppy O'Hanlon had got through to Jazzy with her words. Jazzy understood them and knew that Tash was no real friend. Matt Barker, for all his strangeness, was honest. There was something about him she liked. And whatever it was he had seen in Burnham Wood – if it was real, which it was, she was sure – was something *she* wanted to see as well.

Shakespeare had said it in *Hamlet*: don't close your mind to undreamt-of things. And Jazzy had more belief in Matt's fairy than she had in Tash. So her choice was clear. She was actually on her way to tell Tash (she wouldn't enjoy it, but it had to be done) when, from the disabled staff toilets at the end of the corridor next to the caretakers' room, came an urgent whisper: '*Pssst!*'

The disabled staff toilets were rarely used, since (now Mrs Minchin had left) there were no disabled staff in the school. Also, they were less smelly than the student toilets, which you'd never go into unless you had to. Whoever it was who had called had picked a good place for a private meeting.

But whoever it was had retreated back in, so Jazzy had no idea, as she walked down the corridor, who she was going to see.

She pushed open the door somewhat hesitantly and there, perched on the edge of a basin, like a bird on a bird bath, was Angela Poole. Ange slipped down and smoothed out her skirt before she spoke.

*

'But I *don't* fancy Matt!' said Jazzy for about the third time since they'd started talking.

'Then what are you doing in the woods with him every day?'

'We – have a shared interest.'

'In what?'

Jazzy paused for a moment. 'In trees.'

Ange had a trusting nature, but this was stretching it too far. 'Tash thinks it's more than just trees you're interested in.'

'So what!' burst out Jazzy. 'What does it matter what Tash Lawes thinks?'

'It matters because it's getting to her. She can't let it go. You know what she's like. Something bad is going to happen.'

'It already has!' Jazzy laughed wryly.

'Something worse. If you don't stop behaving like this, she's going to lose patience and really lash out. Then we'd never get back to the way things were.'

'*I don't want to get back!*' said Jazzy.

'Don't want to be happy?' Ange looked truly distressed. 'Don't want everyone else to be happy as well? Like we were before France?'

But Jazzy seemed about to say something unhelpful, so Ange changed the subject.

'Matt Barker's your friend?'

'I keep telling you, yes!' Jazzy huffed. 'But *that's all*.'

'You care about him?'

'Yes, of course, but not like Tash thinks.'

'If you care, you should show him some – empathy – now.'

That was a big Tuesday word. Ange hadn't known it even existed before the Amanda sessions.

'What d'you mean?' said Jazzy.

'I mean you should think of Matt. It's not kind to make him to do stuff that makes him look weird.'

'I don't *make* him do anything!'

'Maybe not. But d'you ever try to help him? Help *him* be happy?'

'He's happy right now!'

But she knew he wasn't.

Maybe Ange had a point.

'What does "empathy" mean, anyway?' she said.

Ange had hoped Jazzy wouldn't ask. 'Seeing things through somebody else's eyes. Kind of. Stepping into their shoes.' She looked doubtful. 'I think.'

Jazzy brightened. 'That sounds like acting! Is that what you mean?'

Ange felt it wasn't exactly, but realized she'd kindled something in Jazzy. So she said, 'Yes. Use your acting skills to stop Matt going back to the wood. Persuade him to give up on – trees – and focus on football. I know you can do it!'

'I wonder . . .' mused Jazzy, but came to a stop.

'It *is* football he likes?'

'Yes, yes.' She stopped again. She was thinking hard. 'There is something I could try . . .' It would be fun, she'd enjoy it – but then she remembered. 'Melissa would probably spoil it, though. She'd see I was acting. She always does.'

'Well, choose a time when she isn't around.'

'She always is. She'd be bound to speak out. She'd give me away.'

They both fell silent. Ange saw Jazzy's excitement fading. She reached for her bag and balanced it on the edge of the basin, to peer inside.

'You just need a way of keeping her quiet, that's all!'

She dipped in her hand and brought out a pale blue ball, the size of a marble (the large kind). 'Take this – she'll love it!'

She handed the ball to Jazzy. 'A gobstopper. Specially designed to shut people up!'

Jazzy eyed it with suspicion, but slipped it into her pocket all the same. 'I'll keep it by me. I may not need it. I'll try straight talking first.'

'Maybe it's time to give up,' Jazzy said to Matt, unexpectedly. 'Maybe there *are* no more fairies. Maybe yours *was* the last.'

She was walking Melissa home from school and they'd bumped into Matt, going home himself.

'You give up,' he said. 'I'm carrying on.'

When caught off guard (except on the pitch), he tended to do this: dig himself in.

'Truthfully, wouldn't you rather play football?' said Jazzy. 'Mikey, Dip, Joe – they like you. They've forgotten what you said on the coach. If you go on like this, they might remember. You'll have missed your chance.'

He knew what she said was true – and he liked what he knew of Mikey, Dip, Joe. He *wanted* to go with them next time they came to the door. Really, he did. But it was true, too, that he was like Hamlet: afraid to take risks.

'Come on!' said Melissa, tugging Jazzy along.

'Lissy, don't pull!' said Jazzy. Then to Matt: 'Oh, all right, then. But you know this is silly. We could end up hurting ourselves. It would be better for you to do stuff with the boys. Better for me –' she swallowed; this truth was bitter –

('Hurry, Jazzy!' said Melissa. 'Nige is making cupcakes!')

'– to go back to Tash.'

'After what she's done?'

'Oh, Tash's all right.' It sounded lame. 'Just a bit confused.'

'Go back to her, then. I can do this alone.'

Jazzy opened her mouth to argue. But they'd reached their houses and Melissa had gone up the steps. She shut her mouth and looked thoughtful. She was fingering something in her pocket.

It wasn't the key.

At last she said with great firmness, 'We'll start straight away. The shift idea. My turn first. But if Mikey, Dip, Joe come round for you, *say yes*. OK?'

Chapter 16

SHIFTY

He couldn't have been home much more than an hour when the doorbell rang. He was in his room, leafing through the pages of *Match*. He didn't put it down, but said to himself, *Maybe they'll think I'm out and try again another day.* He hadn't expected they'd come so soon. He wasn't prepared.

The bell rang again.

He heard Luke's door open. 'God's *sake*! Mum? Dad?' But Matt knew neither was in. There were only the two of them home, and Dash. The bell began ringing a series of long and short blasts, in a mad monotone.

Luke yelled, '*Matt!*' just as Matt worked out it was playing a tune.

Why are we wai-ting? Why-y are we wai-ting? Why are . . .

For the first time, it crossed his mind that it might not be Mikey, Dip, Joe, after all. He hardly knew them, but didn't feel they'd ever ring anyone's doorbell like *that*. They had more patience. (They must have, to keep coming round.) This was somebody else – and at last he guessed who, just as the bell stopped ringing and the door took a battering from a pair of impulsive fists.

'Come on, Matt, I know you're in there!'

Dasher was dancing about in the hall. *She* knew who it was. And when Matt came and opened the door, she greeted the two people standing outside with such enthusiasm that Melissa nearly fell over.

'What are you *doing*?' said Matt sternly to Jazzy. But Melissa was having a coughing fit and Jazzy had to thump her – hard – on the back, till a small pale ball shot out and rolled to a standstill at Matt's feet.

'Gobstopper,' Jazzy explained, as she picked it up. She blew on it briefly and popped it back into her sister's mouth. 'It makes her choke.'

'It makes me—'

'Shh, no talking,' said Jazzy. 'Remember what we said? Don't try to talk till you've sucked it smaller.' Then, to Matt, 'Guess what! You'll *never* guess what!'

'What?' he said.

'We've seen one!'

All this was happening too fast for Matt. 'What d'you mean?' he said. 'Why are you here? You should be in Burnham Wood, doing your shift.'

'What's the matter with you? Can't you understand? We've just *been* there! That's where we saw it!'

'Saw what?'

'*A fairy*!'

Matt looked at her, amazed. Was this how they'd looked at *him* on the coach?

But no, that was different.

Jazzy went on.

She said they'd been sitting at the foot of the ash tree –

'Not me,' said Melissa, and took out the gobstopper, which had turned green. '*I* was doing my den . . .'

'Look, who's telling this story?' said Jazzy. 'You keep

quiet! Put that back before you drop it again.' She gave Melissa a meaningful stare. 'It doesn't matter what *you* were doing . . . *I* was sitting at the foot of the tree, when I noticed . . .'

Melissa sucked hard on her sweet. Jazzy went on, uninterrupted. She had noticed a twig in front of her, she said, begin to shake.

'Was it joined to a branch?' Matt asked.

'No. At least, it can't have been because then it started to rise up into the air.'

It rose, Jazzy said, until it was hovering level with her face, as if it wanted to look her directly in the eye. Her eyes, as she said this, were so wide Matt felt anyone looking directly into them might disappear and be lost for ever. To be on the safe side, he looked away.

Jazzy stretched out her hand and said the twig hadn't been close enough to touch. 'It couldn't, of course.'

'Couldn't what?' said Matt.

'Look me in the eye.'

'Why not?'

'Because *it* had no eyes! They don't, do they? Nor

mouths. Nor anything, really. But they still communicate.'

The twig had made telepathic contact with Jazzy. Her brain had been filled with a lovely, warm feeling of understanding and trust. And then she'd got a clear message: the twig requested that they stop coming. It was grateful for their friendship, but asked that they now please leave it alone. Its future – the future of all the twig fairies – depended on that.

Jazzy paused and stretched out her hand again, as if transported to Burnham Wood and once more in the fairy presence. 'So we have to stop going, like it said,' she concluded. 'Oh, and you have to start playing football – it said that as well!'

'What happened next?'

'It died! Just like yours! It suddenly dropped to the ground!' She let her hand fall to her side.

'Coincidence!' said Matt.

'Yes, that's what *I* thought!'

'Any more?'

'What? Coincidences?'

'Lies.'

No one spoke for a moment.

Then, 'You don't believe me!' cried Jazzy.

'Too right. You forget I *really* saw one.'

Jazzy went red. 'Did you, though? How does anyone know?'

'I said so in the Truth Game! Good job we're not playing the Truth Game now: you'd be out!'

They started arguing then, like two kids scrapping in a sandpit. They didn't throw sand (though they might have done, if there'd been any sand to throw) but they called each other liar and cheat, and each, in their own way, regretted all the time they had spent together. Time which now seemed wasted.

'I can't go on, anyway,' said Jazzy. 'Got much more important things to do. Day after tomorrow, it's the dress.'

'The dress?' sneered Matt. 'The *dress*?' He gave a snort. She was wearing jeans.

She saw him looking at them, and frowned. 'You don't know what I'm talking about! You don't even know what a dress is! Dress *rehearsal*? For *The Tempest*? The play?'

'Well, at least I—'

'*Stop it!*' Melissa had taken out the gobstopper, though she needn't have bothered: it was now no bigger than a pea and wouldn't have prevented her from talking. She was sucking her thumb. And what she chose to say made Jazzy feel anyway she'd been wrong to shut her up.

Melissa stroked Dash, and Dash looked adoringly up at Melissa, who took her thumb out of her mouth in order to say three words.

'We've seen them.'

Jazzy was first to recover. '*There!*'

'Oh yes, and what were they doing?' said Matt. 'Sprinkling fairy dust? Tinkling bells?'

'Give it a break, Matt,' said Jazzy. 'The point is, we *have* seen them, like she said.'

But Melissa said, 'No, not you. *We. We've* seen them. Not you, Jazzy. Just me and Dash.' Then she added, 'No bells.'

'What then?' Matt said stubbornly. 'What *were* they doing? Holding hands, dancing round?' His tone was so sarcastic that Melissa began to cry.

She shook her head. 'No hands,' she said, through her tears.

They looked down at her, crouched over Dash, pushing her face into Dash's soft fur.

'Melissa, you've seen some fairies?'

'I *told* you, Jazzy! Me and Dash.'

'When?'

'All the time. When we go in the wood.'

'What are they like?'

'Like – the wood.'

'What do they do?'

'Don't do anything. Watch.'

'Do they scare you?'

'*No!*' She stopped crying, and laughed instead. 'They're nice! We like them!'

Matt spoke now, for the first time since he'd been mean. 'Will you show us tomorrow?' he said humbly. 'Please?'

But before she could answer, Jazzy objected.

'Tomorrow's the tech run. I mean –' and she said this not in a pointed way – 'I mean, the technical rehearsal.'

'Doesn't matter. It's my shift,' he said. 'Me and Melissa can—'

'No!' cut in Jazzy. 'We all have to go together. We *all* have to see.'

'Well, the next day, then.'

'No, that's—'

'*The dress!*' They said it in chorus, as though this, itself, were a well-rehearsed line in a play.

'Listen,' said Jazzy, 'the whole of next week is *The Tempest*, one way or another. After the two big rehearsals, we perform. First night is Wednesday; last night is Saturday. Burnham Wood will just have to wait. It's not going anywhere, is it?'

'Wait a whole week?' said Matt.

'What's wrong, Hamlet? You're happy to wait to play football! Hey –' she had an idea – 'if you're here all week, they might come for you. You know, come round and ask you to play with them! Mikey, Dip, Joe.'

Matt looked down.

She had another idea. 'I know! Come and watch *my* play!'

'Your play?'

'Well, Shakespeare's.'

'Shakespeare?'

'Oh, Matt, keep up! *The Tempest.* There's still some seats left for Saturday night! I'm going to be Ariel, remember? So that's one fairy you'd definitely see!'

She was going *way* too fast for him now.

'No, thanks,' he said.

Chapter 17

ONE MORE WEEK

Was he tempted to go up to Burnham Wood by himself, while Jazzy was busy with her play? Yes, he seriously was. Jazzy never need know – and he had every right. He'd been taking Dasher up there before any of this. He and Dash could just go for a walk as they used to, before. That's how he'd seen his fairy, wasn't it? If they went now, without any fuss, it might happen again. If he went for a walk.

But he knew he wouldn't.

There were two good reasons why not, though the first he couldn't admit to himself: he was scared. Melissa had said that the fairies *watched*. The idea of being alone in the wood, with them all around, watching, gave him the creeps.

The second was the reason he preferred. He needed someone to show him, someone who saw them better than him. Dash saw them lots. And she'd shown him before – but that had been luck. She hadn't been able to talk to him (of course she hadn't, she was only a dog) but that's what he needed. Someone who saw them and could tell him where to look.

He needed Melissa.

He could knock on the door and ask their mum if Melissa could come out to play *I'm the King of the Castle* on the Burnham Stone. But that *would* be weird.

He couldn't have Melissa without Jazzy, and Jazzy was busy – and that was the problem.

So Matt didn't go to the wood that week.

No one did. It was left in peace. The creatures that lived there went about their business undisturbed. Till recently, they'd been going about it for years, decades, centuries. More than that, even. Building nests, finding food, making good winter stores. And now they had one more week.

And the others, who had no 'business'? Who weren't even 'creatures'? What of them? And who were they? Not birds, badgers, squirrels. Not beetles. Not trees. *Is* there anything else? Besides what you can touch and name?

For sure there is.

You don't often see it (but it does have a name) and it's there,

It was there in Burnham Wood. It had watched and waited for longer than anything else. Far longer.

But it, too, had one more week.

The Tempest was going really well. On Wednesday, Jazzy called Matt in the interval, sounding excited.

'It's great – for a first night!' she said. 'By Saturday night, it's gonna be fab!'

'Saturday night?' said Matt dully. '*Saturday night?*'

'Yes! The last night! You know!'

'Haven't you looked at Facebook?'

'Facebook?' She seemed very far away, and not because she was in the school hall and he was at home. It was more than that. She seemed to be speaking to him from a different world. The things they had shared, in the world of last week, didn't interest her now, not really. Not like this play.

'Facebook?' she said again.

'Yes. Isn't that why you called?'

He couldn't believe it might not be. He closed his eyes tight, to calm himself down.

That afternoon, Tash had pushed things further. On Facebook, she'd put something new. Not a photo. Far worse than that. Far more major. She'd made an event.

BABES IN THE WOOD PARTY

Hey, everyone!

Join the babes!

Meet the spooks!

Burnham Wood, Saturday, 8.00pm

Bring sleeping bags. Plus ones welcome

'Oh, that!' said Jazzy. 'Don't worry about *that*! We'll go after the show. That's why I called. I've got tickets for you and Luke!'

Matt was stunned. 'Luke?' he said. 'Me?' he said. 'Go? *Don't worry?*' He didn't know where to begin.

'I mean, don't worry that they're both on Saturday, Tasha's thing and *The Tempest*. It won't matter if we're late for the party, so long as we go.'

'But I'm not,' he said. 'Going.'

'To the wood?'

'Or the play!' He felt if he kept saying no, he might just be all right.

'But you have to!' Jazzy said simply. 'We have to go to the wood, in case something important happens. It might. And you have to come to the play because you'll love it.'

'Luke won't go,' he said, 'anyway.' That was for sure. He was on safe ground there. And it certainly stopped Jazzy dead in her tracks. It popped her balloon.

'Won't he?' she said.

'Of course he won't!'

'Why not? Is he doing something else?'

'Of *course* he isn't! He just won't go. Why d'you want him to anyway? That's a bit weird.'

It was. And not just a bit. Now he came to think

of it, Jazzy had always been weird around Luke.

'Jazzy, you don't . . . ? Don't tell me you actually . . . ?'

But Jazzy had to go, because something bad happened at her end, she didn't say what. He could hear someone shouting, 'Oh no! Get a cloth!' and then she hung up.

Matt spent fifteen seconds trying to guess what it was, and another fifteen trying to picture Jazzy dressed as a fairy. But he wasn't successful with either, so gave up with both.

If the two of them, Jazzy and him, went to the Tash thing on Saturday night . . . But they couldn't, could they – not together? Jazzy couldn't mean that? If the two of them went – in whatever way – what would *they* think? The fairies of Burnham Wood? Get them to trust us, Jazzy had said. If the two of them went to this party, mightn't the fairies think they had been betrayed?

Best not go.

Besides, if he wanted Mikey, Dip, Joe to give him one more chance (and this time he'd take it), to go would be mad.

Why should he care what happened in Burnham Wood?

Jazzy herself didn't care, he saw that now. All *she* cared

about was Tash: what Tash thought, what Tash told the others to think and whether they'd let her be one of them still.

He wished he'd never met Jazzy. It was all her fault!

Or was it the fault of his fairy? If he'd never seen *that*, then Jazzy would never have come and sat next to him on the coach. The fairies of Burnham Wood deserved what was coming to them on Saturday night, whatever that was. Let them face it alone!

Playing the blame game was almost as good as playing—

Don't say it. Don't get hopeful.

It was all his family's fault, for ever having moved! They'd put him in this position, made him have to begin all over again.

'This is Matt,' the headteacher had said on day one. 'I'm told he likes football.'

So, when Mikey, Dip, Joe had run past him in break time, that very first day, and called, 'Hey, Matt, you coming?' and he'd shaken his head and shrunk back – *whose fault was that?*

Chapter 18
KICKABOUT

For the whole of Thursday and Friday, he never exchanged a word with Jazzy. At school, she stuck closer than ever to Tash: no change there. After school, she was taken up with the play.

Then, on Saturday morning, the bell rang. He'd been expecting it to, sometime soon. She still had to bring round those tickets she'd got. Even though he'd said it was pointless, she wouldn't give up.

What should he do? Refuse to take them? Or take them and throw them away? He could throw them in the King Harold bin, where he'd once thrown the stick. He liked that idea: the two things he definitely wouldn't be doing tonight – both rubbish.

He opened the door.

It was Mikey, Dip, Joe.

Angela Poole was in *The Tempest* too. It was meant to be just Year 10s and 11s, but they needed more sailors for the shipwreck scene and Ange had said she'd help out. Once she'd come forward, they said could she help with a few other things as well, and so it happened that in the magical banquet scene, she was a chair. But Jazzy and Ange were the only non Key Stage 4s. Jazzy had been included because she was better at drama than anyone else in the school.

Both of Angela's parts were non-speaking. The chair was, of course, but so was the sailor. Still, she had stage fright on Wednesday night and was sick in the wings. Jazzy sat with her, trying to be reassuring, while Mrs Montrose cleared it up.

'Can't you just relax and enjoy it?' said Jazzy, who wasn't good at nursing. 'Being on stage is the best thing ever – and it's not like you need to worry you'll forget your words!'

'I didn't know it was going to be like this,' was all Ange would say.

'Just before you vommed, I'd phoned a friend to say how well it was going.' Jazzy wondered how far she could push things. 'I said you were great!'

'Did you?' said Ange. 'Did you really? Who were you calling? Was it Tash?'

'No, not Tash. The point is: everything's fine.'

Ange thought she knew who Jazzy had called, but hoped she was wrong. She'd been grateful for the play as a distraction from all the bad stuff at school: Jazzy was so involved, she'd surely have no time to think of Matt Barker. It was a shame they wouldn't be able to go with Tash on Saturday night, but even that could be a blessing in disguise: Ange felt Tash had something planned and it wouldn't be anything nice. And so she was doubly grateful for *The Tempest*. It was *good* that Jazzy would have to attend the cast party, instead of going to the thing in the wood.

They hardly needed to say why they'd come – it was obvious. But Joe, their spokesman, seemed to think they

should do things properly. So, with neither embarrass-
ment nor aggression, he looked straight at Matt and – as
if the idea were one they'd only just had – said, 'Fancy a
kickabout?'

Mikey, who had long legs, was standing side-on,
one foot on the topmost step of the three leading up
to Matt's door, and one on the bottom. He started to
bounce their ball up the flight – one-two-three – and
then down – three-two-one. Up again, down again, one-
two-three, three-two-one, using his right hand on the
way up and his left, each time, going down. It wasn't a
difficult thing he was doing, Matt thought, but he did it
with perfect control. The smack of the ball on the stone
of the steps never faltered, not even when Mikey changed
hands.

I could do that, Matt thought, and his fingers itched.

He must have relaxed his hold on the door, which he'd
pulled to, behind him, to keep Dash in, because suddenly
out she came, grinning and wagging her tail. She grinned
so much that it made her sneeze.

Dip gave a quiet little sigh, and dropped down on his

knees. He held out his arms towards her and she went to him straight away. When she pressed her muzzle against his face, he laughed softly and whispered something in her ear.

'Is he a boy or a girl?' he asked Matt, the first thing he'd said to him, ever. 'What's his name?'

'Dash,' said Matt. 'She's called Dasher.'

'Bring him,' said Dip and, in an aside, 'Ah, he's smiling! Yes, you are!' Dash sneezed again. 'He can come to the rec. We'll look after him. Won't we? Yes, we will!' He playfully grabbed Dash's ears, in order to look directly into her face.

'Hold her, then,' Matt said – he nearly said him – 'while I get her lead.'

He hadn't said he would go with them, and yet, in a way that they all understood, he had. His hands, as he did up his trainers, were shaking.

'Clip it on to the ring,' he said as he handed Dip the lead. 'The fat one. The one for her disk isn't strong enough. Not that she pulls. But just in case.' He was trying to sound confident, casual, but felt he was making a fool of himself.

He looked to see if they'd noticed, but they hadn't. At the same time, he saw that Mikey was wearing shorts, but Dip and Joe were in jeans, so that was OK, too.

Nobody spoke as they walked down the road, except Dip, who talked to Dash. Whenever she looked up and wagged her tail, he blew her a kiss.

'Sorry about him,' said Joe. 'It's because he's a bit, you know, *deprived*.'

'Of a dog?' said Matt.

'Of a brain!' said Joe, and Dip shoved him sideways, knocking him off balance. Joe went to shove him back and Dip broke away, urging Dash to go with him. Then they all took off together and ended up running the rest of the way.

When they got to the rec, Mikey dropped the ball and immediately kicked it. Matt took Dash off Dip and started tying her to a sign by a gate in the hedge.

'Don't tie him there,' said Dip. 'We're not stopping. We always go down the end. It's too crowded up here.'

It wasn't exactly crowded, but this was the end with the little kids' playground, which meant that a certain number of grannies and granddads and mums and dads with buggies were wandering about.

'Why don't we go through there?' said Matt. 'There's no one through there. It looks nice.' He meant through the gate in the hedge. It stood open and, beyond it, a great expanse of well-kept grass stretched away to a building in the distance. The ground was level, the grass was unworn. It looked lovely.

But Dip pointed up to the sign above Matt's head: 'Granger's Field. STRICTLY PRIVATE.'

'Well, they ought to shut the gate,' said Matt. 'Not everyone can read. Little kids . . . Dash can't.'

'They don't need to,' said Dip. 'No one goes in Granger's. Not even dogs. They just don't.'

'You'd have to be *mental*!' said Joe, coming up. He jogged on the spot, with impatience.

But Matt said, 'Why? What is Granger's Field?'

'Mental hospital!' Joe gave a laugh. 'Full of dangerous psychos. Headcases. You know. Come *on*!'

Matt shuddered, briefly. He took one last look at the beautiful grass, where psychos and headcases prowled, then tugged Dash's lead and ran after the others, glad to be sane.

At the bottom of the rec, he found a slender-trunked young tree to tie Dash to. Mikey, Dip, Joe were kicking the ball to and fro, shouting, 'Over here!' and sometimes, 'Hey! Loser!'

Matt had resolved to play safe, to hold himself back, not do anything fancy. He didn't want to attract attention, just prove his usefulness. He joined them now, wheeling round and about on the edge of things, not diving in. He watched the three of them interacting: they knew each other well.

They were passing the ball between them with ease and sometimes even grace. He saw they were all of them good, though Mikey was best. Joe was a bit of a clown and had bravado; Dip was less showy. They constantly called to each other, mock urgent, but when they called to him, he hung back and wouldn't get involved. It was almost like he was scared of the ball.

Soon they would wonder why he'd bothered to come.

They started tackling each other. Mikey was nicely nutmegged by Joe. His face was a picture, and when Joe and Dip burst out laughing, Matt couldn't help himself: he did, too. And straight after that, Dip backheeled the ball to land right at his feet.

'Matt! Come on! Matt!' they shouted, and one of them (Joe?) added, 'Don't be shy!'

When he touched it, ever so gently, with the toe of his trainer, something happened.

Something strange.

He hadn't been near a football for weeks; he'd been wandering, parched, in a desert, and when he touched the ball that Saturday morning on Burnham Rec, it rained. It didn't actually rain, but Matt Barker was suddenly brought to life in a most extraordinary way.

He *felt* life course through his veins and the whole of his nervous system. It raised the hairs on the back of his neck. It surged through his muscles. It flooded his brain.

He never heard them calling his name after that: he

flowed like a river, flew like a bird – up the length of the recreation ground.

When two of them tried to block him, he wove between them and punched the air. He didn't know who they were, nor where he was going. Those were just details. He was strength, he was speed, he was instinct and skill. That was what mattered. That and the ball. He knew nothing else.

He wove between a buggy and a granny wiping a little kid's nose. The granny was only aware of a movement of air, but the kid really stared. It was like something supernatural had passed by.

The kid let his mouth fall open, and pointed.

Matt came to himself in the middle of a field, with no one around. The whole thing had lasted just seconds, but he was totally confused.

He was standing in this field. Or was it a garden? The grass was so soft and so trim, it was more like a lawn. Fantastic for football. And yet he picked the football up and clutched it against his stomach. He needed reassurance because *now* he knew. He'd never been here before but he knew where he was.

He stood looking round. There was no one in sight. Just a building, a big old house with a flight of sweeping stone steps; cars parked in a car park off to one side; a fence giving way to a hedge, with a gate – an open gate – going through. The sign by the gate faced away from him, of course, but he knew what it said . . .

You'd have to be mental to go in Granger's Field. Well, he'd proved the point. Mikey, Dip, Joe would say he was where he belonged.

A figure emerged from the house, a psycho. It stood for a moment, framed in the doorway, then seemed to spot him.

'Oi!' it called, and began coming down the flight of stone steps.

Run away! Like the scared little pig who cried, 'Wee, wee, wee!' all the way home. Run home, like that.

So Matt set off. All the way to the gate in the hedge he ran, and when she looked back – with one hand on the gatepost, to steady himself – the psycho had come to a stop on the lawn. Even so, Matt wanted to keep going, all the way home.

But he couldn't, could he? He had to get Dash. And Mikey, Dip, Joe would need their ball. He dreaded their reaction almost more than he dreaded the figure behind him.

He could see they were still where he'd left them, though he was too far away to tell them apart. Much too distant to make out their faces. That didn't matter: he guessed their expressions. He knew what *they'd* be. He turned for home.

But what about Dash? He stopped. And the ball? He stood for a moment, nerving himself, then let the ball drop to the ground and began to dribble it – so, so slowly – towards them.

And now he could see that Dip was in the middle, with Mikey a little apart on the left, Joe to the right. He still couldn't see their faces when Dip turned his back and walked away.

It was one of those things that has a completely

innocent explanation. Dip had noticed that Dash had wrapped her lead around the tree. But if you can't *see* the explanation, you have to supply your own. Matt assumed Dip had turned his back in disgust. Quiet, shy Dip, who loved dogs and who had passed him the ball just now – Dip was writing him off. And so, on the spot, he made a decision. Not like just now when something else had taken control and decided for him.

He decided to let himself go. He might as well.

Mikey and Joe had started to move, jogging grimly up the field. It seemed they meant business. He had nothing to lose.

'Dip!' he shouted. '*Dip!*' and Dip turned round just in time to see.

To see the ball come up magically from somewhere behind Matt's legs, climb into the sky and trace a perfect arc through the air. Over the heads of the two attackers it sailed, on its way to the boy and the dog by the tree.

Dip had never seen a rainbow flick and didn't know anyone who could do one. Mikey had tried, on and off, but hadn't come close. The beauty amazed them all. Mikey and Joe saw it start at Matt's feet, with something that looked like it might be a straight backheeler. But as there was no one to pass to, behind – and when Matt called Dip, who was way off in front – they knew it was something else. And when it developed in all its glory, they just stood and stared. First up in the sky, then back down at Matt, standing awkwardly before them.

'Bye, then,' he said. 'Thanks for the kickabout.'

'Bye?' said Joe. '*Thanks?*' but Matt couldn't tell what he meant. If he wanted an explanation . . . Matt shrank inside. An apology, even . . .

'Sorry I ran off like that,' he muttered.

Joe recovered. 'Was it something we said?'

But Matt had had enough. 'Gotta go.'

Mikey stepped out then, into his path.

'You're not going anywhere,' he said.

He squared up to Matt. Matt shrank further into himself. They could do and think what they liked, but he would not fight.

Mikey grabbed the front of his T-shirt.

Matt closed his eyes.

Then something came barrelling into him from behind, surprisingly low, and made his knees buckle so he nearly fell forward. He heard Dip call, 'Dash! Come back!' He kept his balance, but only just, thanks to Mikey, still clutching the front of his T-shirt, holding him up.

He opened his eyes. Dash was dancing around his feet.

Mikey's own eyes were laughing. His face was scrunched up with the effort of keeping the laughter in. Then Joe laughed out loud and repeated the threat, but it wasn't a threat any more.

'You're not going anywhere!' he shouted. 'Headcase! You're joining the team!'

Chapter 19
THE TEMPEST

Deborah and Malcolm Barker heard the front door slam. Dash trotted into the kitchen to let them know she was back. Footsteps went thundering up the stairs and they both remembered a time, not long ago, when Matt would have come in himself, and said hello. His mum sighed. In front of her, on the table, lay an envelope, unopened. She rumpled Dasher's ears and pushed it across towards her husband.

'You tell him, will you?' she said. She sounded tired. 'I haven't the energy. You're better with him. You've got more of a chance.'

Malcolm Barker took the envelope unenthusiastically. He rose from the table, left the kitchen and went upstairs.

He knocked on Matt's door.

'Come in!' Matt's voice sang out at once, from inside.

His dad was so surprised, he said, 'Really?' but he opened the door, all the same.

Matt not only sounded, but *looked* somehow different. Brighter? More alert? He'd got his football down from the shelf and was rummaging round in a drawer.

'I need to pump it up,' he said, 'but I can't find anything in this room any more.'

'Matt,' said Dad, 'I've got something to tell you. While you were out, some people called round.'

It was such a familiar piece of news that Matt caught himself imagining Mikey, Dip, Joe on the doorstep, asking for him. Then he remembered.

'Who?' he said.

'The girls from next door,' said Dad. 'Jazzy, is it? And the little one, whatsaname. They brought this.'

Matt saw the envelope in Dad's hand and said, '*Oh!*'

'Jazzy's in something at school,' said Dad. 'A play. D'you remember, she said?'

'Yes, yes, I know.'

'And she's got two tickets for the show tonight, for you and Luke.'

'Sorry!' said Matt breezily – and that in itself sounded strange to his dad. 'I won't be going. I've told her already. No way.'

Since coming into the room, Malcolm Barker had actually dared to hope. Matt seemed so changed. He'd thought he might say yes. He let the hand holding the envelope fall to his side. Matt saw it and laughed, though not to be mean.

'Nothing personal!' he said. 'Tell you what! I'll go if Luke does. There! That's a promise!' He knew the promise was worthless, but Dad looked so down, it was funny. He felt sorry for him.

And Dad's expression immediately changed. He looked wondering, nervous, and fingered the envelope like it contained something dangerous, over which he'd been told he had power. Matt saw all this, but failed to retract his promise in time.

Dad coughed. 'I hate to tell you, but Luke *is*!'

*

At first Matt thought the hall had been set out the same as it was for assembly. He could see through the door, it was packed with lines of chairs. People were already sitting in some of them, chatting and laughing, mostly parents. Mrs Montrose, the drama teacher, was checking tickets and handing out bits of blue A4 paper, as more people went in.

'Hello, boys,' she said. 'Programme?'

'Yes, please,' said Matt.

She peered at him closely and frowned. 'That's funny,' she said. 'You look different. You can't have got taller since just last week – or can you? I know you're all at it! Never mind.' She shook her head. 'That'll be a pound.'

For a moment, Matt really thought that she was charging him for growing. But as she held out her margarine tub of coins, she was also peeling one of the bits of blue paper from her sheaf, so he worked it out. He hadn't thought to bring any money and guessed Luke wouldn't have, either.

'You can owe me,' she said. 'It's a shame not to know who's who and what's what. This tells you the story.' She gave him the programme. 'I'm on ice-creams in the interval, too. If you come and find me, you can owe me for those as well. It's a shame to miss out on refreshments.'

Luke had already gone in, but Matt said thanks.

Inside the hall, he saw that it wasn't quite like it was for assembly, after all. The stage had been extended to make it poke out right into the chairs. Matt was relieved that Luke had sat down near the back, well away from this new and alarming arrangement.

'Want a go with this?' he said, sitting down next to him, holding out the programme. 'It tells you the story.'

'Nah,' said Luke. 'Read it before.'

Matt stared at him. 'You can't have. I only just got it. From Mrs Montrose.'

'Not the *programme*, dumbo!' said Luke. 'The play! The actual thing. That's what I read.'

Matt was mystified. 'Why?'

Luke shrugged. 'Just to see.'

'See what?'

'What Shakespeare was like.'

Matt hoped Shakespeare was *not* like the story they'd printed in the programme, because that was terrible: a jumble of shipwrecked travellers, all with foreign-sounding names, wandering round an island. Luckily, the lights went out before he could get very far. He thought there had been a power cut, but there hadn't. It was just a sign that the play had begun.

Somebody screamed, a few rows in front, when the first clap of thunder came. (Matt discovered later it was Melissa.) Then flashes of lightning lit the stage, and the hall was filled with the sounds of a violent storm. The stage was the deck of a ship and there were actors skidding about on it, which made it look like the deck was constantly tipping from side to side. Matt saw that one of the sailors was Angela Poole and was surprised, but the way she was leaning her body from side to side, in time with everyone else, was quite good. Everyone else was Year 10 or 11: he knew most of their faces, but not their names.

And then something strange started happening.

Some of the lightning flashes gave glimpses of something weird: a figure that popped up all over the place, contorting itself like a flickering flame and seeming to taunt the people struggling on deck. If they hadn't become more frantic each time it appeared, Matt might have thought he was just seeing things. But whenever it did, the poor, desperate sailors threw up their hands in terror and tried to escape. Angela tripped on a big, painted barrel and fell over backwards, which looked so convincing, Matt wondered if it was meant to happen or not.

The apparition was so unnerving, that when the scene changed to a much calmer one – a father and daughter having a chat on some AstroTurf in front of a cave – it was quite a relief. And then came another surprise. The strange, flamy figure appeared *again* – not so flamy this time, just wispy – and this time it *spoke*. The father and daughter knew it! In fact, it seemed to be under the father's control.

It turned out the father had *ordered* the wispy figure to whip up the storm at sea and frighten the crew of the tossing ship. The figure described the things it had done (which were pretty much what Matt had seen it do) and the father seemed pleased and called it, 'My brave spirit.' He also called it 'Ariel', which made Matt sit forward on his chair and strain his eyes to look more closely.

He peered at the painted, silvery face; he listened

intently to the reedy voice, which was proud when it talked of its recent achievements, but servile and cringing when it feared its master's anger, later on. Matt could hardly believe it. He *wouldn't* have done if he hadn't been told (and if it hadn't been there in the programme).

It was Jazzy.

In the interval, Mrs Montrose was as good as her word. Matt was eating his ice-cream in the foyer outside the hall when all the O'Hanlons (minus Jazzy, of course) came up and surrounded him. Although there were only four of them, they managed to seem like a crowd. That's what they were like.

'Hello!' said Poppy. 'Enjoying the show? Fantastic, isn't it? You look different!' She eyed him suspiciously. 'Had a new haircut?'

Matt shook his head and pointed to his mouth, which was full of ice-cream and partly open, because of the coldness. 'Can't speak,' he mumbled.

'Hope you brought your brother along!' She winked at her husband and Nige, though Matt felt the wink was for him, as well. 'Where is he? Not waiting outside the stage door, with flowers?'

Matt remembered the thought he had had about Jazzy. Jazzy and Luke.

But Luke, he knew, had taken his ice-cream back inside the hall and sat down again with his headphones on. The only door Luke would ever think worth waiting at was a door to a toilet. And he wouldn't know what to *do* with a bunch of flowers!

'Mum!' said Nige. 'Don't tease!' And then, luckily, someone else, another parent, butted in to say how *proud* Poppy and Ant must be. This same person bent down and said to Melissa, 'That's a talented sister you've got!'

But Melissa said, 'I've got a *choc ice*,' and she needn't have even said that, since it was already only too obvious: chocolate was smudged all over her face.

After that, several others came by and said complimentary things about Jazzy. Matt realized he should have said something, too, but felt he had missed his chance. Besides, he couldn't have begun to put his feelings into words. When the play restarted, he found he was waiting for Ariel to appear all the time, and when he did, Matt was filled with wonder again.

Jazzy didn't 'act', like Angela Poole did, nor even like the Year 11 who was really good and played Prospero, the magician (and Ariel's master). When Ange was the chair in the banquet scene, she was Ange in a funny position. When the Year 11, as Prospero, kept getting Ariel to do things and keeping him sweet by constantly promising that he'd get his freedom *soon*, he was good to watch, but you never forgot he was just a Year 11.

But when Ariel dreamt of his freedom and sang a song about himself – about how he belonged with the bees and the bats and the owls – Matt went shivery inside. Of course he knew it was Jazzy, but she had become something else as well.

She was Jazzy *and* she was Ariel, longing for Prospero to release him.

She was two things at once.

And when the play had finished and the actors came back one by one, to get their applause, it seemed to Matt that Jazzy got most. Though possibly that was only because her family were going bananas. Angela Poole got a fair amount, which, as she'd had two of the smallest parts, was much more surprising.

Outside, in the foyer, there were even more people than there'd been in the interval. They pressed up against one another and laughed and said, 'Marvellous!' and 'Terrific!' They squeezed past each other, but instead of 'Excuse me' said, 'Fabulous show!' Matt found himself somehow all mixed up with all the O'Hanlons again. And this time, looking like he wished he wasn't, Luke was, too.

'I'm off,' he said.

But before he could go: 'Luke Barker!' Jazzy herself had turned up. 'So what did you think?'

'Yeah, yeah,' he said, trying to sidle away. 'You were good. You were the best.'

'I didn't mean what did you think of *me*!' exclaimed Jazzy, but under her silvery make-up she blushed. 'I meant what did you think of the show!'

She looked bizarre. She'd changed back into her normal clothes, which were dark and inconspicuous, but because she'd left her make-up on, her face was still Ariel's. It seemed to float in a space of its own, disembodied and even more ghostly than before. It would have been frightening for someone who hadn't seen the play.

'Did *you* like it, then?' She turned to Matt, because Luke had gone. Her mum was trying to congratulate her with a hug, but she pushed her away, saying, 'Careful, you'll get covered in silver!'

Matt said, 'I – loved it,' and Jazzy raised her eyebrows (which were green).

'You've changed,' she said.

He made a joke of it. 'So have you!'

And then the boy who'd been Prospero, still with *his* make-up on (though his wasn't as weird) called across, 'Hey, Jazz, you staying for the party? Lower School hall?'

'Nice eyeshadow!' Nige yelled, and Prospero grinned and made a rude sign and called back, 'Nige boy! Glad you like it – I put it on specially for you!'

'See you later,' said Jazzy, and blew her parents a kiss.

She said she would cycle home afterwards – she'd got lights on her bike, she'd be fine. But when she tried to move off, she fell over. Her legs were stuck together!

Melissa was clasping her round the knees.

'Lovely Jazzy!' she said.

'Lissy, let go! I'm going to the party!'

'*Lovely* Jazzy!' Melissa repeated. 'Can I come? I want to go, too!'

'No, you can't,' said her dad. 'It's a party for people who've been in the play.'

But Jazzy said, 'Well, in actual fact, Dad, they're fairly relaxed about that. We're allowed to bring family and friends. Matt's coming.'

Matt opened his mouth to say something.

('Are you?' said Ant O'Hanlon. 'Good for you.')

He closed it again. He really had changed, like everyone said. He nodded and smiled.

'Melissa can come if she likes,' said Jazzy. 'No one'll mind. She can easily get a lift home at the end. Mrs Montrose will be driving our way.'

Matt waited to hear them say no, it was already way past her bedtime, she was far too young, *of course* she couldn't. Then Melissa would cry and the atmosphere would be spoilt. It was a shame.

But they didn't.

'Look after her, then,' said Poppy to Jazzy, 'and don't be too long.'

What a family! Matt thought. It was something he'd heard his mum say out loud, more than once. His mum had said it with disapproval; he thought it with admiration.

And so the three of them pushed through the crowd – Melissa, Jazzy and him. They kept Melissa between them, each holding a hand so she wouldn't get lost. And all the while, other hands kept reaching out, to congratulate Jazzy. 'Well done!' people called and – if they were going to the party themselves – 'See you there!' But Jazzy said nothing, just smiled and waved.

Because they wouldn't.

When the three of them got outside, they breathed in the crisp night air and turned right, towards the bike racks. They could hear the sounds of the party coming from the Lower School hall, in the other direction. Melissa started to say something, but Jazzy was in a hurry.

'We're going to a *different* party,' she said, 'aren't we, Matt? In Burnham Wood.'

He nodded. He realized he'd known all along that they were.

'And we're not even "going" exactly,' said Jazzy. 'We're just going up there to see what it's like.'

'Can we get Dash, then?' Melissa said happily.

'Good idea,' Jazzy said. 'Dash would be good. Do you think you could sneak her out, Matt, if we go by your house?'

He thought he could. He thought he could do *anything* now, though of course did not say.

And so they got on their bikes, Melissa perched (unsafely, Matt thought) on Jazzy's crossbar. Jazzy wobbled a bit as she pushed off, but they'd be OK, they'd done this before.

And then, as they were getting going, they heard an urgent cry from behind.

'Stop! Please, stop! Wait for me!'

Chapter 20

PARTYGOERS

Angela was limping, because she'd hurt her foot when she'd fallen over the barrel in the shipwreck scene. She looked like the little lame boy in the Pied Piper story, who got left behind. But Jazzy and Matt couldn't think of a reason for Angela not to come with them. She had as much right as them, after all, to go to Burnham Wood. And actually, they were both glad to have one more person on their side. Even if it was Ange. Neither could guess what was coming, but both thought: *strength in numbers*.

Angela had cleaned off her make-up, and now, when they said she could join them, she was so grateful that she offered Jazzy her pack of wipes. It was all she had.

Jazzy said thanks and took it but stashed it away in

one of her pockets. 'I'll keep them for later,' she said. 'I want to be Ariel for a bit longer.'

Being Ariel gave her courage and made her feel strong.

And so it was an odd little group that cycled away from Cufflip School that night, towards Burnham Stone: a girl with a limp (who rode rather lopsided); a boy with unusually quick, bright eyes; a plump little kid clinging on to the crossbar of a bike being pedalled by a fairy! And soon they'd be joined by a little black dog.

They had to ride right through Burnham Stone and almost out again before they reached their own road, and the neat row of new-ish, town-style houses. As they wouldn't be able to cycle with Dash, they left their bikes round the side of the Barkers'. Then Matt went up the steps to his own front door, and opened it softly. He did it in such a way that only one pair of ears in the house would hear.

Dash came out, grinning and sneezing, thrilled to be going on a night-time walk, and Melissa ran up the steps and hugged her. 'We're going to the wood in the dark!' she said.

'Shh!' said Matt, as he reached inside for the lead, then shut the door softly again.

'What will we do when we get there?' said Ange, as they hurried towards Burnham Mount. 'Will we just say sorry we're late? Or what?'

So Jazzy explained all over again. 'We're not really "going" to the party,' she said. 'We'll have to see what we feel, then decide.'

In truth, she had no idea what they'd do.

Nobody did.

Something was wrong. Very wrong.

They saw it as soon as they looked at the sky above the wood. But nobody said anything. And when they got closer, they smelt it in the air.

To give themselves courage, they focused on details. At the foot of the track up the hill, they found eight or nine bikes thrown down all in a pile.

'Hmm, not too many,' said Jazzy, but Matt told Melissa to keep Dash close.

As they made their way up, a cloud slid across the face

of the moon. They pressed tighter together, because now they could *hear* it.

Safety in numbers.

This night should have been no different from the night Matt and Jazzy came looking for Dash. But tonight they had Dash with them and when they found two more bikes at the top of the track, where it went through the wood, Matt reminded Melissa to keep a good hold on the lead.

They could all smell smoke.

Their secret way in had been hacked wide open so it looked like a gaping mouth.

Melissa gasped, and the sound was a welcome distraction from the faint but distinct sound ahead. The one good thing about how the entrance now looked was that Ange wouldn't dirty her clothes getting through, which she might not have liked. But she still wasn't keen.

'It's not really haunted, is it?' she said.

'Yes' – 'No' – 'Not exactly,' said Jazzy, Melissa and Matt all at once, a little too loudly.

It was Matt who'd said not exactly. That was the closest he could get to the truth. He'd have liked to say,

'Oh, don't worry, by far the most evil thing in there is Tash!' But how did he know? The fairies had never done anything bad, but then they'd never been challenged like this. Tash couldn't know what she might be stirring up.

He remembered the tortoise in the story. How it had coldly caused a man's death. And the thought of that kind of magic in Burnham Wood made him feel pretty much like Ange was looking.

'Come on,' he said quickly, before his feelings showed. 'We'll be all right as long as we're . . . *respectful.*'

The people who'd widened the entrance had not been respectful. They must have used knives or even an axe. And they'd used them on the path, as well. They'd ripped through the undergrowth. Jazzy and Matt, Melissa with Dash on the lead, and last of all Ange, moved along it quickly, with that disturbing sound – and the smell – getting stronger and stronger.

They stopped when they came within sight of the clearing, where they could see in, without being seen themselves. And at last Ange said what they'd all of them known.

'It's a fire.'

A dozen people were sitting or lying round a bonfire, which crackled and blazed. It had been a huge one – the new young leaves of the oak tree were badly scorched and the grass round about had wilted and died. Though clearly past its most intense, it still sent up sparks. It lit the faces encircling it, though the wider circle beyond the faces seemed all the more shadowed for that. One figure was standing: Tash. She stood apart, in darkness, near their tree.

'There they all are,' whispered Angela unnecessarily. 'Shall we join them?'

But Melissa said, 'Where's my den? Where've they put my den, Jazzy?'

The fire was burning exactly where the den had been. The den, which had always resembled nothing so much as a pile of firewood itself . . .

'*My den!*' wailed Melissa. 'Make them *stop*!'

'Shh!' warned Jazzy.

But too late.

The people around the fire had heard. One of them turned to peer off down the path, then they all did. Then someone said, 'Ooh-er!'

What they saw was four figures – no, five – the fifth (and tallest) furthest back, most in shadow. But it wasn't that that drew their attention (though it ought to have been). What they fixed on was something silvery, hanging head high at the front of the group.

'What's *that*?' said someone.

A branch in the fire broke in two and the fire collapsed in on itself. Something made a loud pop.

Someone screamed.

It wasn't surprising, Matt thought, that they were scared. He'd been spooked himself. *He'd* been spooked in amongst loads of mums and dads, in the safety of Cufflip main hall. Tash and her lot were seeing the face by firelight. In Burnham Wood.

It wasn't surprising that they panicked.

Jazzy made an odd, ducking movement, then started to sway from side to side. Matt thought she must have gone mad, till he realized she was doing what she'd done in the opening scene of the play.

Round the fire, they were scrambling to their feet.

'What *is* it?'

'A ghost!'

'*Matt Barker's fairy!*'

Even though Matt knew it wasn't, he had an urge to react like them. Their fear was catching.

Kezzia Clay, whose hair was almost as long as Tash's – and who fancied herself as leader if Tash should ever lose her power – saw Tash hanging back and seized her chance.

She would lead them now.

She couldn't go back down the path because that was where the fairy face glinted and turned, so she had to go in the opposite direction. Towards the scrub.

It was shocking to see.

It made Matt wince and close his eyes, even though he didn't like her.

Kezzia flung herself into the thorns.

There was a moment when they held her, like wire in

a war zone, savage and barbed. It seemed she would have to hang there forever, her hair in a tangle, her clothing snagged. Then she struggled and moved herself forward. Perhaps the bushes weren't as dense as they looked. She was dragging herself away – not away from the thorns, but further in, away from the clearing. And the whole time, she screamed.

The others watched in horror, the little group hidden in the shadows round Jazzy and the group huddled bunched by the fire.

When someone does something so desperate, you have to ask why. What made them do it? The group by the fire had no answer to that; they just knew they'd better escape, like her.

'*Come on!*' someone yelled. And that set them off. They began falling over each other to get away. They plunged after Kezzia, yowling like cats, and spent ages thrashing about in the thorns. But at last Burnham Wood had swallowed them up and they'd gone.

And when they had, Jazzy's lot stepped out into the clearing.

Nobody spoke.

They stood and stared into the fire, which had settled, while Melissa clutched Dash for comfort, and sobbed.

'You scared them away,' said Angela at last. 'They thought you were what Matt said he saw when we played the Truth Game in France.'

What Matt *said* he saw. She hadn't meant that. But it didn't sound good. Maybe no one would notice.

But somebody did.

Chapter 21
MACBETH

From the outer darkness, a voice came, sarcastic and cold.
It was so unexpected, Melissa stopped crying.

'Oh yes, so clever, to lie in the Truth Game!' it said.
'And how clever to scare people off with an act! But you
don't scare me, *Jazzy*. You and your face paint!'

They looked towards the ash tree and there, by its
trunk, was the shadowy figure of Tash.

She had not gone.

'Jazzy O'Hanlon!' she said. 'Our fairy! Well, well! And
Matt Barker, our fibber! But *I* know the truth.'

'You let them run into the thorns for nothing?' said
Jazzy.

'You *made* them!' said Tash. She suddenly stopped and

peered past Jazzy, towards the path and the way they'd come.

'Who was that with you?' she said. 'Just now? The tall person? Where've they gone?'

'Ooh, spooky!' mocked Jazzy. 'Now who's telling ghost stories? Let's run away!'

But of course they didn't, and Tash recovered herself and went on.

'You and Psych Boy,' she said, 'going out with each other. My best friend, going out with that weirdo! How *can* you?'

Jazzy's eyes seemed to flash – more brightly than face paint.

'How can *you*, Tash,' she said, 'tell such *lies*? Matt's not weird and we're not going out and—'

'Yes, you are!' Tash interrupted. 'This proves it. Look!'

They didn't know what she meant. They had no choice but to go and see. Tash stood and waited for them. She was holding something in her hand. When the fire flared up for a moment, the thing caught the light and reflected it dangerously. It was a knife.

She took a step back from the trunk of the tree and pointed with the blade. At about shoulder height, they saw something carved in the bark. The fire threw out another flare, and they could see what.

Tash had done a good job. The carving was jagged and crude, but clear.

$$JO'H\ 4\ MB$$
$$TRUE$$

None of them spoke. What Tash had done was *wrong* – and so stupid that, coming on top of the fire and the den, it robbed them of speech. They didn't know where to begin.

Then Melissa started crying again – 'She shouldn't have hurt the tree!' – and Angela said, 'But Tash, it *isn't* true!'

'Is now!' snapped Tash.

And something happened to Jazzy.

It had begun, realized Matt, when her eyes had gone bright. And now it went on.

'Why are you doing this?' she said, very calm. '*None* of it's true.'

Then Jazzy O'Hanlon seemed to swell. Or grow bigger, or taller or *something*. Matt was watching. He saw.

'It's not true that I'm your best friend,' she said, still very calm, but louder now. All Angela's fancy words fell away – what Ange had said in the toilets, how Jazzy had better go back to the past.

She remembered her mum.

'I'm not your friend at all! Never have been!'

And one other word her mum had used.

Matt saw her get *angry*.

Tash tossed her head to flick her hair out of her eyes. But a sudden gust of wind blew it back.

'Hey, guys!' she shouted into the wood. 'You can come out now! Come on!'

But all that came out was another gust of wind.

Then Jazzy made them all jump, by shouting suddenly, '*YES! COME ON!*'

They looked at her, not understanding. Her voice, which she'd learnt to project, made Tash's seem small.

That voice of hers boomed like thunder and rolled away through the bushes and trees, reaching into the deepest depths of the wood. It wasn't natural. Its effect was even more spooky than her supernatural face.

'COME ON!' she thundered. 'ARE YOU THERE? IF YOU ARE, COME *NOW*!'

She didn't mean Kezzia.

There was silence, like someone holding their breath.

Matt held his. He wanted something to happen as much for Jazzy's sake as for anything else. If nothing happened, she'd look silly.

But he needn't have worried. Something did.

After the silence, there came a wind.

This wind made the previous gusts seem like delicate breezes. It rushed at them all of a sudden, hurling leaves and twigs and earth in their faces and blowing the bonfire completely out.

Somebody screamed (this time it was Ange) and then something happened deep in the wood – but coming towards them.

Deep in the wood, Ange's scream was echoed. Echoed and amplified. It was nothing to do with Ange, really, nor any of them.

It wasn't *human*.

It was the wind, the voice of the wood.

Everyone knows wind can whistle and howl; this was nothing like that.

It screamed, as Ange had screamed – only not like that, either. It screamed and bore down on them and was more frightening than anything else they'd heard in their lives.

And then it was upon them. In front and behind, all around. *Inside*.

It got right into their heads, and scattered their thoughts like so many useless scraps of paper.

Even Dash pressed her ears flat back and quivered and showed the whites of her eyes.

A big branch high up in the ash tree broke off and came crashing down beside them. It brought smaller branches with it.

They all jumped back.

Except Tash, who jumped forward – into the thorns – plunging crazily after her friends.

But the others jumped back – and Melissa let go of the lead.

'DASH!'

As soon as she felt herself free, though, the dog was gone. Melissa cried out once more and then followed, and now the other three did as well. Even Jazzy, whose anger had started it all – who had seemed in command – was overwhelmed. They went the same way as Melissa and Dash. They could have gone back, but they didn't. They hurled themselves into the cruelly whipping briars, trying to find paths where there weren't any, trying to catch up with the dog and the child.

Trees creaked and cried out. Branches thrashed.

Burnham Wood raged.

They found it wasn't true that there weren't any paths. There were ways through the wood – if not paths exactly – that they could take. And so, amid all the tumult, they moved forward. Each found their own way. It was hard and it hurt and they sometimes had to drop down on hands and knees. And always the terrible sound of *anger* was in their ears.

But they forced themselves on.

Matt half crawled, half rolled into a hollow and got entangled in some ivy. He managed to tear it off – it wasn't spiky – and tried getting on to his feet. But almost at once he fell forward and hadn't the strength to get up again. Bleeding and exhausted, he lay on his back and looked hopelessly up at the stars.

The stars.

He could see the sky!

He was out in the open.

Beneath him, the ground was rough: a farmer's field. It sloped up away from the wood and, encouraged by this, Matt pulled himself on to his feet and stumbled forward. He kept falling over, but got up again each time. So, very slowly, he made progress up the hill. And as he went, he began to get a sense of his surroundings and to hope he'd be safe if he reached the top. At the top was Home.

But would 'Home' still be there? It might not be, tonight.

If it wasn't . . .

If it wasn't, he was done for. There'd be no protection. No refuge at all.

But it was.

More ancient than the wood itself, what could shift the Burnham Stone?

He collapsed on it in relief and after a while found he had enough strength to raise himself up on his elbows and look back.

And so he saw what happened. Nobody else did, no one else had his view. He had to describe it all afterwards, only this time there was no problem: they believed him.

Here's what he saw.

The wood went all round the hill. From his position on the Stone, the sound of the storm below was faint, which wasn't surprising. But he rubbed his eyes to clear his vision because he should have been able to focus – there was plenty of light from the moon out here in the open – but he couldn't. The trees seemed to him to be *seething*. He thought he must have been staring at them too hard. The thick, black band that stretched round the hill seemed unstable, no longer fixed.

And then it was as if someone had done a tracing of Burnham Wood, and shaded it in with a good, black pencil – and then started sliding the tracing away. That was how Matt described it. The wood seemed to lift away from itself. It was there on the hillside still, and yet it was sliding, slipping away.

It was two things at once.

Burnham Wood was itself *and a smudge of itself* moving up the hill.

If it reaches me, Matt thought helplessly, what then? I'll have to go with it, I'll have no choice. Stone or no Stone. He wouldn't have minded so much yesterday, but now . . .

How sad to leave *now*. They'll find me here, he thought, but the smudgy bit of me will have gone. He imagined them lifting his body, limp and cold . . .

In the beginning, Jazzy had pictured the fairies amassed, rising up to claim their stick. And what was the word she'd used?

Was this the spirit of Burnham Wood, coming up the hill?

Maybe.

Whatever it was, though, it never claimed Matt.

Perhaps the Stone stopped it; perhaps it didn't. Whatever, before it got near him, it lifted away and grew less distinct. If anyone else had seen it (which Mrs Montrose did, on her way home from the party at school) they'd have thought that a storm cloud hung over Burnham Mount.

Mrs Montrose was sure she'd be using her windscreen wipers before she got home, but oddly the rain never came and the cloud dispersed.

Burnham Wood was still there, of course. Woods don't move. But what was it Jazzy had said – long ago – about *that*? There was a play – a different play – in which one did.

And now there was movement below him again, but only something small. He squinted. Something detached itself from the wood and began to crawl towards him, up the hill. A small ant-like creature, moving painfully slowly. Now it stopped, as if too weak to go on – but no, it was coming on now, once again. And when it had stopped and started a few more times, he saw its face glinting silvery white in the light of the moon.

But it wasn't silver *because* of the moon.

It was Jazzy.

She was really weak: she could only move by going on hands and knees. Or perhaps she was really strong, since she wouldn't give up. Matt didn't feel he himself had the strength to help her. But on she came. And at last, breathing hard, she made it and hauled herself on to the Stone, beside him. There was just room for her to lie flat on her back. She closed her eyes.

'You all right?' he said, but she seemed to have fallen instantly asleep.

Matt closed his own eyes.

The two of them slept a strange sleep on the Burnham Stone, with only the moon to see. It doesn't matter how long. Jazzy's mouth was open and she snored in a comical, gobbling way, which didn't matter, either, since nobody heard. Eventually, one of her snores was so loud that she woke herself up.

She opened her eyes. She ached and tingled all over and the skin of her face felt unpleasantly greasy. She remembered Angela's wipes and got them out. When she broached the pack, the sound of the seal unsticking woke Matt.

'You all right?' he said, as if repeating the last thing he'd said, without having slept in between.

Jazzy didn't answer, but worked in silence on her face. She was still lying flat on her back, and when she'd finished, she flung her arms wide. Luckily, Matt had sat up, or she'd have thumped him.

And when she spoke, it might or might not have been to answer his question. Her face was back to normal now. The bunch of wipes in her hand was smeared with the silver make-up she'd taken off. And her voice was normal, too, not like it had been in the wood when she'd summoned that wind.

'Now my charms are all o'erthrown, and what strength I have's mine own.'

The words were somehow familiar but . . . 'Ariel never said that,' Matt objected.

'No, Prospero did,' said Jazzy. She laughed. 'Next time, I'm gonna be him!'

Chapter 22

AWAY WITH THE FAIRIES

Ange was the next one out of the wood.

She emerged further round than they'd have expected, and much further round than they themselves had. She'd done really well to get so far. Matt was impressed.

'Up here!' called Jazzy, and waved.

Angela didn't wave back but she did start picking her way towards them, up the hill.

She didn't wave because she was carrying something in her arms. It was big enough and heavy enough to put waving – even briefly – out of the question. That and her foot, which still looked like it hurt, meant she made slow progress.

Whenever she stumbled on a lump of earth, she held her bundle away from her body, as if to protect it in case she fell. And yet it wasn't alive; when she was close enough, they saw she'd taken her coat off and used it to wrap the thing completely, like a parcel. And she didn't fall, either. When she stood before them at last, she was shivering – being only in a T-shirt now – and her hair was a mess, her skin scratched, but she didn't have mud on her from the field.

'What's that?' said Jazzy, pointing to the bundle.

But Angela didn't respond with words. She responded with a look, and it was an unusual one for her. It was an appeal. Ange, who liked to be helpful and kind to others, for once looked at Jazzy and said with her eyes what she'd never said before (though maybe she should have done): 'Help *me*!' She didn't look at Matt. Without explanation, she started to cry.

For a second, Jazzy was puzzled. Then a shock went through her. She leapt to her feet, although not to help Ange.

'*Where's Melissa?*'

Then she was running, arms flailing madly to keep her from falling, down the hill.

And Ange was left holding the baby, as they say.

But it wasn't a baby.

Out of one end of the bundle, something familiar hung uselessly down.

A dog lead.

Having been torn by thorns in the wood, Ange was now torn by indecision. Should she go after Jazzy or stay with Matt? Still without meeting his eye, she held out her wrapped-up bundle towards him and he took it in his arms, as he sat on the Stone, and laid it gently in his lap.

He bent his body protectively, like a bird with a clutch of eggs. He folded the bundle into himself.

'Sorry,' said Ange. Then again: 'I'm sorry.'

But she might as well have been talking to the moon. So she left him and ran after Jazzy, who hadn't yet quite re-entered the wood.

'Not there!' she shouted. 'Go further along! I've been through that bit – she's not there!'

*

The two of them, Jazzy and Ange, forced their way through the wood from about where Ange had appeared. The wood had calmed down. Their calls were the only – at least by far the loudest – sound there.

'Melissa! Melissa!'

'*Lissy!*'

'Where are you?'

'Come out!'

But they got no answer and so they crashed on.

At one point, something quite large – a fox or a badger – fled noisily through the undergrowth off to one side and Jazzy stopped dead in her tracks. But it wasn't Melissa. At another, an owl hooted suddenly overhead, but obviously that wasn't her. And at last they burst out, through some specially dense bushes, into open ground again. Only they weren't in the field above the wood, nor on the slopes below. They were on a track going through it, a second track, which they hadn't seen before.

But if they'd never seen it, how come Jazzy (in an odd, back-to-front kind of way) began slowly to think she had?

She looked across to the tangled hedge on the opposite side – and there was a gaping hole.

'It's *our* track!' she exclaimed. 'We've come right round!'

They were back where they'd started. By turning left – and then right, at the top – they would see the Stone. By turning right straight away, and heading downhill, they could go home. Which is what Tash's lot must have done, since the bikes they had left up here were gone, and so were the ones at the bottom, it seemed.

'Let's keep going,' said Jazzy.

'But we've been right round,' said Ange. 'Like you said. We know she's not in there. She must have gone home.'

'She hasn't gone home,' said Jazzy. 'She wouldn't go home by herself.'

'But—'

'*She hasn't gone home.*'

So they crossed the track and re-entered the wood. Angela couldn't see the point. They followed the newly widened path, and so, pretty soon, they came to the clearing again.

*

The fire was out.

Of course it was. But the moon was enough. Enough of its light reached into the clearing to show what was there. Sleeping bags, all messed up on the ground, and one, which had been caught up by the wind and thrown on to the thorns, hanging limply like someone dead.

There were one or two bits of litter, as well, and a few discarded garments.

And a little mound of clothing under the tree.

Including shoes.

They could see a shoe poking awkwardly out to one side.

And it had something in it.

A foot.

The mound at the base of the tree was more than just clothes.

If Ange had been with them the night they found Dash up here, she might have thought this was a replay. Jazzy went forward, as Matt had done then (though without his hesitation). Ange herself stayed back and watched, like Jazzy, before.

Jazzy knelt over the unmoving form.

She gave a sharp, thin cry.

And Angela turned aside and threw up in a bush.

If Ange had been with them the night they found Dash, she might not have been surprised by what happened next.

Jazzy cried out again and the mound of clothes *moved*. Jazzy raised it up in her arms and a pair of arms came out and went round her neck.

'Have they gone?' came Melissa's voice, high-pitched and fearful. 'Jazzy, have they?'

But Jazzy didn't answer, just hugged her tight.

So Ange stepped forward. 'Yes, don't worry, they've gone,' she said reassuringly. 'It's OK. They won't come back. We can build you another den tomorrow.'

Melissa's head popped up suddenly then, from some-where behind Jazzy's shoulder.

'Gone?' she repeated, her mouth a startling black hole.

She looked about and her eyes were two dark pools of desolation.

When Angela saw those eyes – that's when she knew there was more to this than she'd thought (and she'd known it was all a bit weird, to say the least, even to start with). Afterwards, when Matt talked about it, she kind of understood. She remembered the strange words Melissa spoke next, and she thought they made sense.

'Gone! All gone!' Melissa was sobbing. *'And left me behind!'*

When they came out on the track again, there was a blue flashing light at the bottom.

'The police!' gasped Ange in terror (though luckily managed not to be sick this time). 'They've come to get us! What shall we do?'

'Go down and explain,' said Jazzy. 'Or, at least, go down.'

And so they did.

The three of them walked down the track hand in hand, with Melissa in the middle. The police weren't the only ones waiting for them: they didn't stop till they'd walked right into the open arms of their parents. Poppy and Ant O'Hanlon. Ange's poor mum, white as a sheet.

But Deborah and Malcolm Barker saw it was useless to hold out their arms.

The Burnham Stone was cold but, wrapped in Angela's good winter coat, Dash's body felt warm. Matt did not cry.

She liked them, he said to himself, over and over, and rocked the two of them, her and him, gently this way and that. *They made her happy.*

He pressed his face into the folds of the coat. He was nuzzling one of her ears. In the dark and the warm, it was just him and her.

Him and his dog.

But he knew that the coat belonged to Ange. She would need it back. And night would in time become day.

But right now . . .

Dash's ear was a lovely soft flap. Underneath it, his lips barely moved as he whispered, 'Hey, Dash.'

He felt for the clip of the lead and undid it.

The lead fell away.

Then he whispered again: '*Hey, Dash. Have fun.*'

Chapter 23

A MATCH

Everything changed after Burnham Wood. How could it not?

When you find that the world isn't how you thought it was, you can't stay the same.

Jazzy discovered strength. She'd always been strong and now she was stronger. (After Burnham Wood, she did something she'd never have done before. You'll see.)

Tash discovered fear, and Ange discovered a bit of both.

Oddly enough, it was Matt who changed least. But perhaps this wasn't so odd. He'd changed already.

So not quite everything changed after Burnham Wood. Just everything *nearly*.

Tash never took her lot up there again. They weren't even really 'her lot' any more. You can't go on being a leader if you spend your time being scared.

Matt never went up there, either, because . . . Well, for various reasons.

But Jazzy still went.

'Sorry, my love,' said Poppy O'Hanlon when Matt rang the bell one fine May morning. (She'd taken to calling him that.) 'I'm sorry, she's out. Gone up Burnham Mount. To the Stone, I should think.'

Matt could have just gone home. But he had something really important to say and it might be good to have a reason to go up Burnham Mount at last. Besides, on a morning like this, it was hard to feel sad.

He tried not to look at the clumps of tall grass on either side of the track. But when it went through the wood, he looked at the place in the briars and thorns which had been hacked open. The briars and thorns had already started growing back. By summer, he thought, the gap would be gone. At the top, he came out of the wood and took the path that ran up the last little bit of the way, by the side of the field.

He saw at once there were two people up on the skyline.

Although they were just silhouettes, he knew who they were. They were standing together, on top of the Stone. And as he walked up towards them, one of them, with a dramatic gesture, suddenly pushed the other off. The one who'd been pushed ended up out of sight, in the wheat.

The one on the Stone was Jazzy. She stood, feet apart, hands on hips, head thrown back. It was *I'm the King of the Castle* – and the Dirty Rascal retaliated by sending up sprays of earth from the field. But they weren't much good.

When Matt arrived, Jazzy was laughing and Luke (because that's who it was on the ground) was clumsily brushing earth from his head. He'd managed to throw it over himself, instead of her.

'Look at him! He's so *funny*!' said Jazzy.

But Matt shrugged, not seeing it himself. People said Jazzy and Luke were a perfect match – both his parents thought so, and Poppy O'Hanlon had said so, loudly, when she'd come round on Luke's sixteenth birthday. Matt didn't get it.

He shrugged again.

Luke scrambled to his feet. His jeans were all chalky from having sat down in the field, but he seemed not to notice. He didn't say hi to Matt. He turned on his heel and shambled away down the path.

He didn't say bye.

'See you, then!' Jazzy called after him. 'Have a nice day!' Then, to Matt, 'He's hilarious! He really cracks me up!'

Matt couldn't agree. So he just said, 'Come down from there, will you?'

He hadn't set eyes on the Burnham Stone since that terrible night. It seemed another time and place that he'd sat holding Dash in his arms. The Stone in bright spring sunshine looked totally different. But still, he'd have liked to have this conversation somewhere else. And besides, when he tried to look up at Jazzy, the sun got in his eyes.

But Jazzy said, 'No, I'm not coming down. I like it up here!'

He had to shade his eyes with his hand when he spoke to her again.

'There's a match tomorrow.'

'Football?' she said.

'Yes. Cup Final. We're playing.'

'Well, I hope you win.'

Something else that had changed since Burnham Wood was that Burnham Barons, the under-14s team, had started to do really well. Last year they hadn't but – amazingly – now . . .

'If we win, we'll be the best.'

'Then I really, *really* hope you do.'

She really did. He heard it in her voice and decided to chance it.

'You should come.'

'Me? Football?' she said.

'Yes, come and watch. We're playing at home.'

'Watch a football match? *Me?*'

He had made a tactical error. He, Matt Barker, who'd rescued the Barons by pure, sheer genius on the field, had timed it wrong. Her voice had changed. But he couldn't go back, so he went on. 'Why not?' he said. 'And there's something else. We're playing in Granger's.'

She burst out laughing. 'Now I *know* you're joking!'

'I'm not. This match is such a big deal, we want to promote it.'

Des, the Barons' manager, had approached Granger's about their Field. Granger's had liked the idea. It was just the kind of outreach they needed.

'That's mad!' said Jazzy.

'It's not,' said Matt. 'They want to reach out.' He didn't care what he said now. 'They want to reach out to the community. Change their own image and people's perceptions. But *you* wouldn't know about that.' He paused. He wasn't good at this and didn't know whether he'd made himself clear. 'You wouldn't know about seeing anything with new eyes.'

Jazzy ignored the attack. 'Will *they* be there? Watching?'

'Some of them. Maybe.' It hadn't occurred to him that they might, but why shouldn't they? It was their Field, after all. 'If they like football. So what?'

But Jazzy just said again, '*Mad!*' and looked down on Matt with enormous eyes full of twinkling amusement.

And suddenly Matt was furiously shouting.

'*I went to your play!*'

Which shut Jazzy up. For a second or two.

Before she came back with: 'That's totally different! You *totally* can't compare football with Shakespeare!'

'Why not?' shouted Matt. 'I can if I want! What makes you think Shakespeare's above everything? He isn't!' And before she could answer he added, 'Nor are you!' – and he pushed her, rushed up and gave her a whacking great shove, so she toppled off the Stone.

Chapter 24

SEEING WITH NEW EYES

Someone is walking down Burnham Rec on their own, with (for once) unsure steps. They're walking beside the hedge, towards that gate.

The sun is shining. The gate is open. The person walking is Jazzy.

They'd taken down the Strictly Private sign and put up another:

WELCOME TO GRANGER'S FIELD
FOOTBALL MATCH 2.00 PM

CUP FINAL!

BURNHAM BARONS V TARBURY WOLVES

It was 1.45 and already there was quite a big audience.

(Was that the right word? It was right for the theatre, but wasn't there something else you used for football?)

Anyway, they stood in groups at the edge of the pitch, admiring the pristine grass and the crisp, newly painted white lines. Some were the parents of Burnham players and looked familiar; others did not and had probably come to support the Tarbury Wolves.

There might even have been a few who hadn't come for the football at all, but just to get inside Granger's Field at last, and see what it was like.

There *might* be Granger's inmates – Matt had said so – trying to get out! (He hadn't said that, but they might be, why not? That was much more dramatic!) Only all the spectators (yes, *that* was the word) seemed happy, standing about in the warm spring sun.

The truth was you couldn't tell who was who, and there could be all kinds of reasons, apart from the obvious, why people were there. One group (who clearly *was* there for the obvious) was conspicuous by its size. Mikey's family had turned out in force: parents, grandparents, one or two cousins, an auntie, and Mikey's twin brothers, who not only looked the same as each other, but also like miniature versions of him. His mum looked up from helping one of them undo a bottle of water and noticed the newcomer: 'Oh! Hello! Come to watch? Lovely day for it! Stand with us if you're on your own.'

And when the players, who'd been milling about at some distance, came on and got organized, one of his granddads (there seemed to be two, one quiet and one noisy) shouted, 'MIKEY! SHOW 'EM, MIKEY! GO ON!'

Mikey was one of the two who faced each other in the middle, at the start.

'Did you know they made him captain?' said his mum to her new companion. 'Yes, they did, at the start of the season.' She was trying to sound casual, but her pride showed through.

Then the referee blew his whistle and they were off.

The Barons were in red (it was easy to work that out because Mikey was); the Tarbury Wolves were in blue and white stripes. But within their teams, as they raced here and there, the players all looked the same. Only the people in goal stood still. The Barons' goalie was Joe. For some reason, Dip was standing with three or four others under the trees, just off the pitch.

There was *lots* of racing about – and one or two blows of the referee's whistle, which made it stop for a moment, while everyone regrouped.

And suddenly someone yelled, '*Matt!*' and a figure in red was running amazingly fast down the field.

'Matt! Matt!'

Was it him?

Yes, it was. Him and the ball.

Somehow he kept on running, though people kept trying to stop him and nearly succeeding.

'MAN ON! MAN ON!' shouted Mikey's granddad madly, whenever that happened.

Mikey himself sounded much more calm, when he called, in his captain's voice, 'Steady, Matt! *Steady!*'

He was like the director – which probably wasn't a football word. But he *was*.

'You can do it, Matt! In your own time!'

And Matt did.

He shot, and the ball flew towards the goal. The Tarbury goalkeeper lunged for it bravely – and missed – and the ball went in.

Mikey's granddad went mental. If there *were* any people from Granger's, they had nothing on him. He made the players themselves look very low key: a few just patted Matt on the back as they passed, on their way to take up their positions again.

'Dad! Calm down! You'll give yourself a seizure!' said Mikey's mum, clapping. And then (not to him): 'That new boy's great. You know him? He must be about your age? Mikey says he's really turned things around.'

Just before the interval (no – wrong word again – Mikey's mum called it 'half-time') there was a moment when the ball was coming straight for them, all the Maloneys, and looked set to wind up in their midst. The twins even started arguing over which should kick it back. But neither did, in the end, because two players were on to it just before it could cross the line. They skirmished right there for it, so close up, you could see the studs on their boots. A big fierce Tarbury boy, who flared his nostrils and breathed like a bull – and Matt.

Suddenly Matt was Matt, not just somebody racing around in red.

But he *wasn't* quite Matt. There was something about him. The eyes were Matt's eyes; the mouth, lips drawn back as he fought for control, was Matt's mouth. But quiet, reserved Matt Barker never made faces like that at school.

Nor at home, sitting chatting, on the edge of his bed.

He was different now.

He was two things at once.

Every muscle, not just in his face, was strained: his legs had become somehow huge. And he seemed unaware of anything other than this troublesome opponent. The spectators, though almost as close, might as well have been distant clouds in the sky, for all the notice of them he took.

'Matt! It's me! Look! *I've come!*' But he seemed not to hear. 'Look! New eyes!'

And then it was over. Matt did something technical with his foot and the other boy did something back but it wasn't enough and the ball was suddenly flying away from them both, to be received by one of the Barons, who took it away.

'TAKE IT AWAY!' Mikey's granddad yelled, but that's when the whistle for half-time blew.

'Put one of these in your mouth, Dad, and let's have some peace and quiet for a change!' Mikey's mum started handing out sandwiches: cheese-and-pickle, just cheese, or ham. 'Take one, go on,' she pressed her new friend. 'We've got plenty.'

It might have been open day for Granger's Field, but it wasn't open house. The building with all the windows overlooking the grounds seemed closed up, same as ever. But you never can tell.

Two men, one old and one young, were working their way along the line of spectators, pausing to chat now and then, before moving on. They paused at Mikey's family, and the old one said, 'Got any really strong cheddar?'

'As a matter of fact, I have!' said Mikey's mum, getting out the box.

'No, really,' said his companion. 'He's only joking.'

And clearly he was, because his face, which had had a caved-in look before, was now utterly scrunched up with laughter. 'Forgot to put in me teeth this morning!' he spluttered. But almost at once, he recovered and said with great seriousness, 'It's a very good game!'

'You're right, sir, it is,' said Mikey's granddad.

'And I'll tell you something for free (though you can pay me if you want) –' another quick face scrunch – 'that lad who scored is one to watch!'

'Right again! And let me tell *you*: so's their captain!'

'Dad!' exclaimed Mikey's mum. 'How many times? It's not good to *brag*!'

But the toothless old man didn't seem to have heard. 'I'll be on the blower tonight,' he went on. The young man beside him plucked at his sleeve. 'I'll be on the blower tonight and I'll tell them to watch that lad who scored. And they'll take him on – you see if they don't. They listen to me!'

'Who?' said Mikey's granddad.

'Chelsea!'

Mikey's granddad guffawed.

The young man started leading the old one away. The old one didn't seem to mind being led – nor that Mikey's granddad had laughed at him. 'You see if they don't!' he repeated, sounding confident and happy. And as they were going, the young man turned to Mikey's mum and whispered: 'He's harmless, but he needs his head examined. Don't you worry. *I've* got contacts at Man U!'

Not far into the second half, Tarbury scored and then scored again. Mikey's granddad and everyone clapped, but only out of politeness, and the second time round you could almost hear them forcing themselves. The old man and the young man, moving on down the edge of the pitch, had just drawn level with a couple of spectators who clapped so half-heartedly that they made no sound at all. They stood in silence, with anxious faces. The men didn't stop for a chat.

'There's still time,' said Deborah Barker to Malcolm. 'Let's look on the bright side. It's anyone's game.'

'That's what I'm worried about!' said Malcolm.

Both of them knew how much this meant to Matt.

To relieve the tension, Deborah looked up and down the line of spectators.

'Look!' she said. 'Isn't that . . . ? Yes, it is! Well I never! Over there, standing with that big group . . .'

'Who?'

'Jazzy O'Hanlon!'

Malcolm looked where she was looking and saw, yes, Jazzy, but something else, too. In that instant, a change came over the group: they all started jumping about like popcorn. Two little boys broke away and did cartwheels, and an elderly man gave a woman a hug and finished by throwing what looked like half a sandwich up in the air.

Something had happened on the pitch.

Deborah and Malcolm looked back, but they'd missed it. People were clapping in frenzied excitement.

Mikey Maloney had scored a goal.

Deborah and Malcolm clapped louder than anyone else and Deb mouthed to Malcolm, *Two all!*

*

Jazzy felt she could have settled for that: no winners, no losers, just four good goals and one of them Mikey's, one Matt's. She had seen it all.

But no, she hadn't. Just as Mikey's granddad looked at his watch and drew in his breath and said, 'Five more minutes!' Matt got the ball as he had before, and took it down the field.

But you couldn't catch Tarbury twice the same way. They had seen what Matt could do, and now they were ready. They bore down on him, a ruthless pack, to block his path. Even their goalie came forward, out of the goal mouth, scenting blood.

Jazzy felt someone gripping her arm. It was Mikey's mum.

Matt stopped, seemingly uncertain, but did not pass.

And then it happened.

Only two people on the pitch – and one of the subs, waiting under the trees – had seen it before. Nobody else. Not Mikey's granddad (in all his born days, as he put it later), not the two men from Granger's – and of course not Jazzy.

And even the three who had seen it before hadn't seen it like *this*.

The ball traced its effortless arc through the sky and landed in goal.

Poetry in motion, people said, didn't they? Jazzy had never understood what they meant.

But watching Matt's rainbow flick, she kind of did.

It made her think of a bird in flight, one of those ones that drop into the sea from impossibly high in the sky – and come up with a fish.

It made her think of words so precise and so perfectly combined that they blow you away.

She could hardly believe it had happened, but . . .

There are more things . . .

She could hardly believe this was happening to her.

It was poetry, yes.

It was beautiful, powerful, true. All that.

There are more things in heaven and earth . . .

It's like Shakespeare, she thought.

Chapter 25

'CLOSURE'

Mr McGann was puzzled. He sat in the staffroom, not talking to anyone, letting his mug of coffee go cold. He'd been like this for days. That's an awful lot of wasted coffee.

'Ted, you look puzzled,' said Mrs Montrose, sitting down in the chair beside him.

'What?' he said absently. 'Oh. Yes. That's right.'

'What's up?'

'Eh?'

'What's wrong?'

He seemed to hear her at last.

'It's my Key Stage 3s. They're different.'

'How do you mean?'

'I don't know. That's just it. They're happy enough, most of them. Jazzy O'Hanlon . . .'

'Ah, Jazzy. It isn't surprising *she's* happy. Something's suddenly clicked and she's going for it now. That girl's got a fabulous future in drama if she keeps it up.'

'Well, I'm glad to hear it,' said Mr McGann, 'but there's something they're none of them talking about. Something else. Not even her. There's an *atmosphere*.'

'Who else have you got? Tash Lawes? She's a bit of an atmosphere specialist, isn't she?'

'Yes. Or – she *was*. Have you seen what she's done? That's part of it. Something's happened. It's as if there's a cloud . . .'

Mrs Montrose remembered a certain, strange cloud she had seen from her car. But she knew it had nothing to do with Mr McGann's, which was only a metaphor, so she kept quiet.

'How's Matt Barker?' she asked. 'Has he settled in now?'

'Yes. He's fine. No worries there. He's found his footballing feet. He and Dip Jay have become thick as thieves.'

'And Mikey Maloney and Joe? Do they mind?'

'Only too happy to have him, I think. I gather he's rather a star on the pitch.'

The two teachers fell silent.

Then Mr McGann started frowning again.

'I'll tell you a funny thing, though, and I'm sure I'm right – I've been watching them closely. Tash Lawes is *nervous* around Matt Barker. In fact, I'd go further: I'd say she's afraid.'

'You don't think it's—?'

'Bullying? No! Matt's no bully, I'm certain of that. He minds his own business. But here's something else. *Someone* else she's afraid of. You'll say I'm mistaken, but I know I'm not. Jazzy O'Hanlon.'

Mrs Montrose drew herself up. 'You need a holiday, Ted. You're letting things get to you now. Imagining things. If it's a bully you're after, Jazzy's would be the *last* name on your list. No, wait! It wouldn't be there at all!'

'Oh, I don't know what I'm after!' Mr McGann sounded suddenly tired. Maybe Hilda Montrose was right about him. There were too many weeks till the end of term.

'If I was after a *victim*, I'd hardly have started with Tash – in the old days. But now . . . It doesn't make sense.' He paused. 'But you're wrong about Jazzy . . .'

Mrs Montrose pursed her lips and prepared to get tough.

'There's one other person,' Mr McGann went on, 'Tash Lawes is avoiding, and *she* really *is* the last person who'd ever intimidate anyone else.'

'Who's that, then?' said Mrs Montrose.

But before he could say, they both heard a tactful cough and somebody else said: 'Angela Poole.'

They looked up and saw Miss Inshaw, one of the student teachers, hovering close by.

'Ahem,' said Miss Inshaw again. She wasn't alone. She had Ange by her side.

'Angela wants to speak to you, Mr McGann.'

'*Miss Inshaw!*' said Mrs Montrose, in her most severe voice. She'd been all set to use it on Ted. 'The staffroom is Strictly No Entry To Pupils! Have you forgotten?'

Miss Inshaw became confused and started steering Angela Poole away. Ange herself seemed relieved. 'I tried to tell her!' she said.

But, 'Come back!' called Mr McGann. 'This is silly. You're here now. Thank you, Miss Inshaw. Now, Angela, what did you want to say?'

Gratefully, Miss Inshaw left them and Mr McGann gave Ange his best smile. 'What brings you here, to talk to me, then? Not an ill wind, I hope?'

Far from being reassured, Ange seemed startled. 'A wind?' she said, looking anxiously round.

Mrs Montrose knew how she felt. There were too many metaphors altogether this morning. 'It's a figure of speech,' she said kindly. 'It's an ill wind that blows . . . Oh, never mind. I'd better leave you two alone.' She began getting up.

'You don't have to go, Miss,' said Angela. 'Stay, if you like. That would be fine.'

So Mrs Montrose was drawn into the story.

Ange turned to Mr McGann. 'I came to tell you – I mean, to ask you . . .'

Mr McGann took a sip of cold coffee, to fill in the gap before Ange tried again.

'Could we – I mean, I'd like to . . .' She looked round once more.

Mrs Montrose smiled encouragingly and Mr McGann said, 'Yes?'

'We need to play the Truth Game,' said Ange. 'In French!'

'In *French*?'

'Well, not *in* French, but in a French lesson.'

'Oh!' But that wasn't the problem in Ted McGann's mind. 'It's not long ago that we played it before!' *And we nearly came unstuck then!* he thought. 'If you play the Truth Game too often, it starts not to work.'

'It'll work,' said Ange. 'I promise. It's the only thing that will. You see –' and she used a word her mum used a lot, one of Amanda's favourites – 'we need "closure".'

Mrs Montrose raised her eyebrows.

Mr McGann said, 'Well, I don't know.'

'You won't be sorry,' said Angela. 'Oh, *please*.'

And suddenly Mr McGann knew she was right. The Truth Game was *just* what they needed.

Mrs Montrose was gazing at Ange with new eyes.

She hadn't distinguished herself in *The Tempest*, not in a good way, this girl. She hadn't been anything much to write home about. But she seemed to have changed.

Watching her now, Mrs M was thinking: *What a remarkable child.*

When Mrs Montrose walked into Ted McGann's classroom, she thought at first that everything looked OK, if a little surprising. But Ted had warned her about the seating arrangements he allowed for the Game. Tash Lawes and her girls were grouped at the back, some perched on each other's knees. A bunch of boys were off to one side, all sitting on chairs, except for Matt Barker, who had brought his football and was sitting on that. Angela Poole was on her own, at the table nearest the teacher's, and Jazzy was up on a cupboard, drumming her heels on the front, claiming centre stage. *That's my girl!* thought Mrs Montrose.

But who was that new girl, off in the corner, all by herself and looking as though she'd like to disappear? Her head was shaved and her eyes were downcast. What a sight. Why had Ted McGann not mentioned *her*?

And then he called for silence and she looked up.

Mrs Montrose was deeply shocked.

The girl in the corner with the shaven head and the haunted eyes was Tash Lawes.

'Silence!' called Mr McGann. 'That means no noise! Taisez-vous!' He pointed at Jazzy – 'Tais-toi!' – and her heels stopped drumming. 'Everyone looking at me now,' he said.

Mrs Montrose sat down on the chair next to Ange.

She knew she shouldn't, but she *had* to: she twisted round in her seat to look at the group of girls at the back.

There was Tash Lawes!

But no, not Tash Lawes. With her long, blonde hair cascading down over her straight, upright back, she'd just looked like Tash for a moment.

It was Kezzia Clay.

'Any questions?' said McGann. 'Before we begin . . .' It was part of the ritual.

Kezzia glared defiantly back at Mrs Montrose.

'Why's Miss here?' she said.

'Ah,' said Mr McGann. 'I was coming to that . . .'

'Has she got a story?'

'Well, no, not exactly, but she heard we were playing . . .'

Mrs Montrose intervened. 'I'm just an observer, Kezzia. I'm intrigued by this Game and was wondering if I could use it in drama. But as I have nothing to contribute, I'll quite understand if you'd like me to go.'

'What do we think?' said Mr McGann. 'Any objections? To Mrs Montrose sitting in? Angela, you don't mind, do you? Jazzy?'

Jazzy beamed and gave him a thumbs-up sign.

'Kezzia?'

He didn't ask Tash.

Kezzia shrugged. 'I'm not bothered.' It was more than off-hand. It was downright rude, and Mr McGann had to take a deep breath.

'Perhaps you'd like to start off, then?' he said coldly. 'I'm sure going first won't bother you, either.'

But at that she bridled. 'Ange said *he* would go first.' She tossed her head towards the boys. 'Said she'd fixed it. With Matt Barker.'

Mr McGann had to fight back a feeling of not being

the one in charge here. He glanced down at Ange and she nodded and smiled.

'OK, Matt, you're first. Do you want to stand up?'

He did, but he picked up the football, too, and clutched it tight while he spoke.

He, too, looked at Ange before opening his mouth.

Then, 'I saw a fairy,' he said.

There was silence.

Uh-oh! thought Mr McGann. *Déjà vu!*

Even Ange had a moment of doubt. *What if it's Groundhog Day?* she thought, and got a familiar feeling in her stomach.

And Mrs Montrose? She was just plain amazed. The Truth Game was nothing like how she'd imagined. She didn't know *what* to think, except that Angela Poole looked horribly much like she had just before she'd thrown up in *The Tempest*.

But Ange wasn't sick.

And this silence was different – different to the hostile one that had followed Matt's opening line on the coach.

It didn't go on, either, because very soon he was speaking again.

'I saw a real live fairy,' he said. 'The day before France. It happened like this.'

He told the whole story from start to finish. He told about him and Jazzy researching and then sitting under the tree. He told about Tasha and Facebook and how it had ended. Ended for all of them. Ended for Dash. And when he stopped, there was silence once more. No one even put up their hand. But then they did.

Mr McGann was in no state to make a decision which one to choose. For no special reason, he went for Joe.

'*Now* I get it!' said Joe. 'It was live when you saw it, *but already dead when you picked it up*!'

Joe liked to get things straight, and this had bothered him ever since France.

'Why did - *they* - leave?' said Kezzia, even though Mr McGann hadn't picked her. 'Was it because of what Tash did? Was it Tash Lawes's fault?'

'Oh, not necessarily, no!' said Ange quickly.

But a voice from the top of the cupboard said, 'YES! IT WAS!'

They all looked at Jazzy, expecting more. But she let the accusation hang in the air.

And off in the corner, a chair was pushed back and clattered on to its side.

They all looked at Tash.

Tash had got to her feet. She'd lifted her hands to her head, to cover her ears. Her eyes were still down. She kept them like that as she made for the door.

Nobody tried to stop her. Not Mr McGann. Not Mrs Montrose.

And when she'd gone, nobody followed.

The sound of the door banging shut behind her hung in the air, as final as Jazzy's own words that had hung there before.

But now Jazzy went on.

'It *was* her fault,' she insisted. 'But –' she raised a finger – 'not *just* hers.' She pointed at Kezzia Clay. 'Yours, too!'

Kezzia started to say something.

'And mine. And Matt's. *Everyone's*. We all charge

round ruining things, and then we wonder why things go extinct. We're surprised nothing stays!'

'Have the fairies gone forever?' said one of the girls. 'Won't they ever come back?'

'No idea,' said Jazzy. 'But I doubt it.'

And suddenly everyone seemed to be shouting. Jazzy had whipped them all up and they weren't going to bother taking turns.

'How do you know?'

'Can't you tell them we're sorry?'

'Were there lots, or just one big one?'

'Could they have killed us?'

'Sorry about the dog.'

Mr McGann had never seen anything like it. But then, whenever they'd played before, there'd never been one truth that everyone shared.

He stopped himself: this was no truth!

The Truth Game was spoilt.

Matt Barker had told them a tale and Jazzy O'Hanlon, with her acting skills, had got them all going.

This was a hoax!

But he had an ally. He looked at Mrs Montrose. He knew an abuse of trust when he saw one – and so would she.

The room was still full of shouting.

'*Was it fairies making that noise in the wood?*'

'*Were they angry?*'

'*Where did they go?*'

Mr McGann held his big French dictionary high above his head and let it fall flat on the floor at his feet.

BANG!

And in the sudden hush a voice that had not been part of the shouting spoke up.

'I know where they went!'

It was Mrs Montrose.

Everyone looked.

Everyone waited.

Mr McGann felt dizzy and had to sit down.

'At least, I know which direction! I saw them from my car!'

Chapter 26

BACK TO THE WOOD

Autumn. Summer has been and gone. Luke came top in all his exams, except one: English lit. (He didn't turn up for it.) He's at sixth-form college now, though he's still going out – whatever that may or may not amount to, Ange still doesn't know – with Jazzy.

Jazzy's rehearsing for another Shakespeare play: *All's Well that Ends Well.*

Nige is in sixth form, too, and glad to be able to change his image. To be honest, though Tash never worked it out, he likes boys, not girls.

Tash's hair is growing again, but she won't ever be the same.

And Matt?

Well, it's autumn and a fine, bright day. Two boys are making their way up Burnham Mount. The track is covered with damp, yellow leaves, which one of the boys keeps kicking in the air. The other is kicking a football, trying to dribble it uphill, through all the leaves, which is hard.

'Give us that here!' said Matt. 'Let me have a go. You're not on the pitch any more! You got to accept these conditions are different. Adapt.'

He side-stepped across to Dip and, with just the toe of his left boot, tweaked the ball away. Dip had no time to protest.

'Hey, leave off, fairy!' he said, but way too late.

They called Matt 'fairy' sometimes; only because of his footwork, though. Now, for example, he was dribbling the ball uphill through the drifts of wet leaves, for all the world like he was on AstroTurf with no leaves in sight.

He stopped when the track went into the wood and waited for Dip to catch up, with his foot on the ball. Dip came to a stop beside him and peered uncertainly into the trees.

'D'you think you can find it?'

'Dunno.' Matt shrugged. 'Haven't been here since . . . Haven't been here for ages. Maybe.'

He started forward again, but dribbling more slowly now, scanning the undergrowth on their right. Dip did the same, just behind him, but both of them knew, if either was going to find the way in, it had to be Matt.

'That's it!' said Matt suddenly, stopping.

'Where?' said Dip.

'No. I mean we've passed it. It's gone. Overgrown or something. I knew this would happen!' He was almost relieved.

'Then why did you come?'

Why had he? He'd never brought anyone else, hadn't even been back on his own. (Mum had said wouldn't he like her to come and plant flowers, but he'd said no.) But over the summer, he'd done loads with Dip – and Dip had loved Dash – and he'd got the idea of bringing him here. To see.

And Dip had seemed keen, in his quiet, Dip way.

But now he was barging into him, not quiet at all, trying to get the ball.

They fought for it, hard, and at last it got booted away, ahead of them, up the track. It disappeared into the bushes and Dip ran to get it. Matt stayed where he was.

And suddenly Dip was shouting excitedly. 'Hey! Over here! *I've* found it!'

'You can't have!' Matt called back. 'That's too far along. My way in was down here!'

'*Your* way, yes! But I've found another! Come and see!'

It turned out the *ball* had found it – though no one could miss it who came this far. The ball was sitting in the middle of a track that hadn't been there before. Branching off the original one, almost as wide and newly cut, the farmer must have cleared it, to get a vehicle into the wood. It wound invitingly here and there in amongst the larger trees.

'Come on!' said Dip. But Matt didn't want to.

It was too unexpected.

'Adapt, remember?' said Dip, and led the way in.

This path made Matt sad. It was so very different from the old one. And not only that, the whole wood was different. It wasn't surprising, really: now *they* had gone, it was bound to be – less. So when he heard Dip exclaim, 'Found it!' again – 'I've found the clearing! It's just like you said!' – he didn't hold out much hope.

But it was.

The new path had brought them in at a different point, but not that different. And the clearing itself wasn't that much different from how Matt had seen it last. The leaves were yellow, not green any more, and they carpeted the ground, but the sun still filtered in through the boughs of the ash tree. The tree was still there.

'Nice place,' said Dip.

Matt went forward to where he'd stuck the twig in the ground. To mark the spot. Not *the* twig, of course. Just a twig he'd picked up when he'd finished the job.

He hadn't wanted anyone there to watch. Melissa would only have cried (and if she hadn't, Ange certainly would have) and inviting Jazzy along would have been as good as inviting Shakespeare. Shakespeare was bound to have something to say about death and digging graves, and the last thing Matt needed was a speech.

He'd wanted to bury Dash without words.

He'd wanted to dig on the spot where she'd barked at the fairy, that very first time.

But the tree roots made it impossible, so he had had to move further away. That didn't matter. But even then, it had been hard work to dig a deep enough hole.

And afterwards, when he had filled it in, he couldn't get the earth to go back to being flat: he was left with a mound, which he hardly needed to mark, though he did anyway.

But the twig had gone now. Not taken by fairies. No, just fallen over, like any twig would, if you left it for weeks and weeks, stuck in the ground.

And now it was lost in the autumn leaves.

But Dip had spotted the mound.

'Is that it? Is he under there?'

Matt nodded, unable to speak.

'Nice place,' Dip said again, quietly.

He came to stand beside Matt and bowed his head.

They stood like that, side by side, for quite a long time. Then Matt broke the silence.

'Dad went to look at a litter of puppies,' he said.

'Awww! Puppies!' said Dip straight away.

'He went this morning. He says we could have one.'

Matt didn't know how he felt about that. He waited for what Dip would say.

But Dip was silent. Perhaps he'd not heard.

Matt started repeating the statement, then stopped. What if Dip was *too shocked* to reply? He became aware that Dip was taking unusually quick, shallow breaths. And then – it came out as hardly more than a breath itself – Dip whispered something.

He wasn't in shock.

What he whispered was, '*Lucky!*'

So Matt carried on. 'Dad says we might get a boy this

time.' He glanced at Dip's face to catch his reaction. 'Just for a change.'

But again there was no reaction.

Dip was like someone in front of a picture, staring and staring, allowing the picture to draw him in. His eyes were all dreamy, his breathing still quick. Then, again, he came out with a single word, the one he'd come out with at first.

'*Puppies!*'

And suddenly Matt was smiling. He couldn't help it, he was so *glad*. Glad he'd brought Dip, glad Dip was OK about the idea. Because he was, too.

Now he knew.

He was smiling and smiling, feeling relieved that no one could see.

Dip couldn't, lost in his picture. Which was lucky.

And that was what Dip had called *him* just now. Lucky.

Or had he?

What – *who* – had he meant?

For a moment, Matt, too, got a picture in his mind

and was drawn in, himself. Though his wasn't of a whole litter, but just one puppy, who sat on a blanket. The puppy's tummy was round, its paws a little too big and its ears a joke. But it looked back at him with confidence and cocked its head.

Lucky, you and me both, it seemed to say.

'Come on,' said Matt, and the smile was in his voice, as well as all over his face. 'Let's go home.'

Their figures and their voices receded as they went back along the new path. Dip had come out of his trance and was overflowing with excitement.

'What kind of puppies? How many? *When* will you get one? What will you call him?'

Matt did his best to answer the questions. He answered the last, to his own surprise, most easily of all.

But by then they were out of earshot, too far away for the name to be heard by anyone lingering behind.

After they've gone, the clearing is quiet. A squirrel comes to poke about in the leaves and a little brown bird flits across overhead. Then something frightens the squirrel and it bolts up a tree. It runs straight up the trunk of the ash, just like that: like the trunk is a highway and running vertically upwards is as easy for squirrels as running along the ground. Perhaps it is.

On its way up, it passes some marks cut into the bark, but they're old, unimportant. No one would notice them now, unless they were looking for them, but nobody is. Nobody's been here over the summer and the marks have almost gone.

The tree is unhurt.

And there's something else, too.

Come further in, where there aren't any paths.

Come in and see.

Deep in the wood there are briars and brambles tumbling and tangling together. And at this time of year, there are rosehips and blackberries; bright red haws on the hawthorn trees.

Come in and look at the autumn colours. The reds of the haws and the hips – though actually some are more purple than red, and some orange. And look over there, at the sloes, with a dusting of ripeness which makes them look blue.

And there: there's an elder tree festooned with sprays of little, black, shiny berries. And next to it an alder – but *is* it an alder? – all hung with clusters of much more unusual-looking fruit.

Ever seen these before? Each one is made up of four plump blobs stuck together and dangling down on a thin, straight stalk.

They're lovely, these fruits – not to eat, but to look at, at this time of year.

And their colour? What would you say? It's not obvious.

Pink?

No, not really.

Red? Scarlet, perhaps?

Too dark.

Well, what then?

Pale crimson.

Something has gone from Burnham Wood, it's true. The wood has changed.

But that's what woods do. This isn't the end. Burnham Wood has a *viable future*.

I'm going now, not leaving, but going further in. And you'll want to get back. We'll part company, then. But as you go, just look over your shoulder.

There are so many different kinds of spirit. Glance over your shoulder. You might see – me.

I'm the one Tash saw and Matt half-saw.

Or half-thought he saw. Way back when. With Dash.

Disappearing into the trees.

Author's Note

When I wrote this story, people were talking about ash dieback disease. (They still are.) It seemed that ash trees were on the way out.

This story isn't just about trees, but readers who like explanations for things may choose to interpret it partly as my farewell to the ash.

Acknowledgements

Thanks to Joe Lever, my football consultant,
without whose invaluable insights
this book could not fully have come to life.